The Giraffe Has Fallen

An Eighth Day Village of the Sun Saga

by Nick Delmedico

Published by

Copyright ©2025 by Nick Delmedico

Contact: halfabook@dplus2.com

All characters in this book are fictional; any resemblance to persons living or dead is purely coincidental or has been granted by permission. The Eighth Day Village of the Sun and New Maya City of Worlds are also fictional, created by my good friend Randall Rex Harrison, a man who believes that intentional communities are the next step in human growth and development. At the time of publication these places do not exist, except perhaps in our hearts.

Manufactured in the United States of America

The Giraffe Has Fallen

New Age Fiction

Action and Adventure

ISBN 978-1-58884-026-4 (print version)

     978-1-58884-027-1 (eBook version)

Introduction

In writing this book I asked a lot of people, including two Artificial Intelligences, the essential question "When you think of God, what do you imagine?" This work is a culmination of the answers I received, along with my own philosophy. I dedicate this book to God and to the many manifestations God takes.

All writers hope to spread their ideas. Next to telepathy, reading and writing are the best ways to communicate ideas. And so, I keep writing, even if it's just my journal, a passing poem, or a tattered note. Writing somehow brings out the depths we hide inside ourselves. It speaks the language of the soul and magically translates it to the human experience. It reaches out to touch others. Just ask anyone who has crafted or received a thoughtful, well written letter to or from a relative or a dear friend.

So, whatever you write, keep writing. Whatever you read, keep reading. Whatever you think, keep thinking and exploring. May you find God in your heart, in your prayers, and in your life.

I believe there are as many ways to God as there are people. And so it is. God bless you!

Thank you.

Nick Delmedico

May 2025

Chapter 1

Is There Hope in Desperation?

Kamala Singh's gait was less than graceful as she nervously made her way down the narrow stone corridor. The temple had many dark places like this, places she had been hesitant to explore. Until now.

Her cueitl skirt caught on a rough stone. She let out an angry curse, tugging at it until it ripped at the hemline. She pulled it up with her hand, inspecting the damage. "No matter. I'm tired of wearing this stupid costume." She let go of the skirt and continued down the dimly lit corridor.

A high priest appeared out of the blackness ahead of her. "It is an honor. You wear the traditional clothing of the High Priestess of the Temple of Ascension."

"I don't care what it is," she said. "I won't be wearing this outfit much longer. I never wanted to wear it in the first place. I look like the star of a cheaply made Bollywood movie." She stopped and reached under her shirt, grabbing at the heavy, gold inlaid bra. With surprising strength she yanked it off her chest and threw it to the ground. "And you have no idea how much it hurts to wear this." She threw her head back, a sigh of relief that sounded like the last breath of a dying dragon.

"Please don't do this, Kamala. You have no idea..."

"You're just a ghost," she said, moving forward again as she quickened her pace, her arm extended defiantly towards the priest. Her hand touched his chest and disappeared into it until she had walked through him and emerged intact on the other side.

The priest turned as she exited his back, shouting warnings and talking about abominations and acts against God, nature, and humanity.

A young ghost appeared beside him, this one garbed as an ancient Toltec. "Listen to our father," he called. "He did not teach you the ways of the temple so you can do this."

"Be quiet, Ixpetz," said Kamala, ignoring them both.

"But I am a part of you," he said. "We all share the same soul. You, me, and Papaitl here are all one. You must hear us out."

"Not for long," said Kamala. "When I complete this process, I will be free of you both."

"But not of the Golden Being that is your soul," said the high priest Papaitl. "Your brother is right. Please stop and think about what you are doing."

"You are not my father, Papaitl," said Kamala. "You are only the forgotten priest of this temple. You died long ago."

She reached her destination. The corridor opened slightly, a shelf in the wall appearing beside it. It contained a narrow track with a large mirror able to slide across it. Reflected light from the mirror focused through a lens and then traveled down the shelf and into a hole. Kamala moved the mirror, turning it to direct the light down a different track. The whole area lit up, an intense beam that illuminated the walls of the shaft. What had appeared to be imperfections in the stones were now visible with writing, a warning from time gone past.

"Now you did it!" said Papaitl.

"Shut up!" said Kamala, turning and walking through the ghosts of her history.

Papitl and Ixpetz looked at each other. "What do we do now?" asked the old priest.

"We can try to move the mirrors."

"Impossible," said Papaitl. "Our ability to influence people is the only power we have over the physical world. We cannot touch or hold anything."

"Perhaps we can influence one of the temple guards," said

Ixpetz. "Or perhaps even a lesser priest or clergy."

"It's too late, my son," said Papitl. "She is determined. When she reaches the sacred chamber of the Ascension Crystal it will be all but done."

Ixpetz swung at the mirror, his hands passing through it. "Please don't give up hope father," he said.

"Everything in the world exists though a balance of opposites," said Papitl. "The Crystal is capable of extraordinary things. It can consciously connect the flesh to the spirit, even elevate it to the level of the soul. But it is also capable of the opposite. Kamala thinks she is unlocking the greatest secret to ascension, but she is about to destroy her life."

"And our lives as well," said Ixpetz. "We have no idea of what will happen to us."

"Yes," said Papaitl. "And there isn't a thing we can do about it."

"I'm not sure," said Ixpetz. "I believe there are others who can help. Let's go find them and see if I'm correct."

Chapter 2

The Sea is Forever Changing

Barclay McKenner lightly rested his hands on the wheel of the boat. The seas were calm and his grip just as gentle. He liked driving the boat. He enjoyed piloting everything from boats to aircars to giant crystal airships. It gave him the illusion that he was in control of something. If only he felt that way about his life.

His friend was standing beside him. "We're getting close," said Franklin Van Dorn.

McKenner let out a sigh. "I know. I can feel it." He closed his eyes for a moment.

Monica was seated behind them enjoying the boat ride. With her strong psychic senses she could feel something too, but then, anyone could sense the strong emotions and gloom leaching out of Barclay McKenner. It was pasted on his face like cheap wallpaper, peeling and cracking for lack of anything holding it together.

"Hey! Pay attention," said Van Dorn. "Open your eyes. You don't want to run into a reef or something."

"Don't worry," said Barclay. "I know this area well. I used to live here. Remember?"

"Stop that," said Franklin. "I'm sorry. It kind of freaks me out that you were recently turned into a dolphin and now back into a human."

Barclay opened his eyes. "How do you think I feel about it?"

"I don't know," said Franklin. "You haven't talked about it much. How *do* you feel about it?"

McKenner scanned the horizon, lowering the speed of the boat until it dropped off the plane of the water's surface. The solar charged electric jet boat belched a gentle stream of bubbles behind it as it glided towards a mooring buoy. Van Dorn saw it, caught it with a boathook and secured it in place with a line.

Barclay McKenner silenced the motor as he let go of the wheel. He stood behind it and stared down at his hands. He jiggled his fingers.

Monica gave him a curious look but he didn't notice. He was sad but not frowning. His mouth was flat and his expression empty.

"No sign of the pod," said Franklin as he looked out over the flat sea.

The sound of his friend talking pulled him out of his quiet reflection. He closed his eyes and concentrated. "No, they're not here today."

"Do you know where they are?" asked Monica.

He focused, trying to use his deeper abilities. After a moment, he opened his eyes and shook his head. "No." He went back to scanning the horizon.

"What do you feel?"

"I'm not sure," said McKenner. "I'm lost. It feels like I've lost something and I'm not going to find it again."

"What have you lost?" asked Monica.

"My connection to the dolphins for one thing," he said. "I used to sense where they were, even before I became a dolphin. Now I sense..." His eyes closed again as he whispered. "Nothing."

"It has been strange," said Franklin. "We've been coming out here looking for days and haven't found them. Usually we are overrun with dolphins wherever we go. What's different now?"

"Me," said McKenner. "I'm different. I don't feel the connection to them anymore. They must feel like I've abandoned them."

"I know you had a child with Valencia while you were a dolphin," said Franklin.

"Yes. I lost my dolphin family too. I would like to see my son again," He stared at the distant sea, light reflecting on the surface. "And my wife, Valencia, too. I'm sure she misses me."

"No doubt," said Monica. "Why don't you want to talk about it? I'd like to try to understand what you are feeling."

"Because I can't quite describe it," said Barclay. "I'm left with a strange emotion, one I can't quite grasp."

"Emotions don't need to be held or grasped as you put it," said Monica. "They are part of our humanity. They just need to be experienced."

"Don't put too much faith in that. Being human is not all it's cracked up to be," said Barclay.

"What was different when you were a dolphin?" asked Franklin.

"Meditation for one thing."

"Ah!" said Monica, nodding in agreement. She looked towards Franklin. "We were in a group meditation while Barclay was a dolphin. He and I and some others. I know what he's talking about. Think about it, Franklin. You meditate, don't you?"

"Of course," he said. "Every day."

"Okay. Imagine yourself a dolphin."

"It's not like I haven't done that before." Van Dorn closed his eyes and thought. Barclay already had his closed, following along with her.

Monica spoke softly, her words helping them visualize the experience. "First of all, there's less gravity. You're floating in the ocean, weightless in an environment that gently supports and presses against your body."

"I love the feeling of the water against me," said Van Dorn, his eyes still closed. He took a deep breath.

"Yes," she said. "As a dolphin, you don't need to breathe as much. You can go fifteen minutes between breaths if you want."

Franklin reached out with his mind. His breath slowed, trying to imagine what it must have been like for his friend, trying to visualize himself as a dolphin.

He felt a gentle touch on the back of his neck. "You breathe through here," said Barclay.

Franklin tried to imagine it. He was used to feeling his breath move in and out of his mouth, tracking where it went as he distributed prana, the mystical life force in the air, throughout his body. He focused on a small space on the back of his neck, trying to imagine his breath moving in and out there.

"Now you make a high pitched dolphin noise, your sacred mantra. It opens up a higher dimension and you not only sense Ascended Masters and angelic beings, you also see them."

"See them? How?" whispered Van Dorn.

"I can't say exactly," said McKenner. "It's like some kind of high frequency echo location. The right pitch can call them to your side."

"Ah," said Monica, reflecting on how she could use her psychic abilities to sense the presence of such beings. "Yes! Attune yourself to the Ascended Masters," she whispered. "And slip into a deep meditative state."

They all had their eyes closed now. The boat rocked gently, the current making it tug against the mooring buoy. The gentle sound of the waves lapping against the side was soothing. Barclay re-experienced his meditation as a dolphin for a moment, a lugubrious flashback to a life he had only begun to explore before he was cut off from it.

Somehow, just as he had gone from being a human to a dolphin, he unexpectedly went back to being human. There were advantages to both forms. There were things he could do with fingers that he couldn't do with fins. There was the ability to swim with powerful muscles. There was the way he was able to join with Valencia, his dolphin mate, and produce a child.

"Prospero," he quietly whispered.

"Prospero," repeated Monica. "Who is that?"

"My son," whispered McKenner.

Van Dorn ended his brief meditation. He looked over at Barclay McKenner. A sadness descended on him, joining his friend in mourning for what he had both gained and lost. The boat rocked gently, the sound of loose gear and rubber bumpers rhythmically breaking the silence like a dirge of bells at a funeral.

It was Monica who brought them out of those depths. She stood up and took off her shirt, pulling her hair together as she reached for her mask and fins. "Well, I hope we didn't come all this way just to stay dry. The reef here is fantastic. Pod of dolphins or not, I'm going in. Now, who's with me?"

Chapter 3

The Enraged Goddess

Kamala Singh stormed into the room that was the Ascension Chamber. The giant crystal glowed in the center of the room, fed with sparse light from shafts that were tuned with mirrors. The ancients found that they could control the frequencies and filter the sunlight by changing the lenses and the distances between the mirrors. The temple was honeycombed with shafts and hallways that performed this function.

There were grooves along the walls where large circular stones could be rolled aside to access some or all of the light tunnels that terminated in the Ascension Chamber. The Crystal rested on a pivot point and could easily be rotated to allow a certain ray to break its surface and enter it at a designated angle. On the floor surrounding it there were markings that indicated specific positions that would optimize the Crystal for different effects.

Upon sight of her, two guards snapped to attention. "Mistress," said one of them. "Oh, look. You ripped your skirt."

"Get out of here," she demanded.

"We will not leave our post, even for you Mistress," said Kovax, the larger of the two. "We were appointed by the New Maya City of Worlds Council of Elders to guard the Crystal and keep it safe."

"It is safe with me," she said. "Am I not the high priestess of the temple?" She went to one of the circular stones along the wall and rolled it aside. Sunlight streamed into the chamber. The Crystal glowed brighter, the room lit in a rainbow of refracted colors.

"You're not supposed to do that," said Kovax. "We have our orders. The Crystal must not be moved, illuminated, or disturbed.

We do not want to repeat what happened before."

"The Council acts out of fear," she said. "They do not have the knowledge and understanding of the Crystal that I have."

"But it is their job as the Governing body to keep everyone safe," said Kovax. "Perhaps they act not out of fear but out of concern for the population. In either event Mistress, I must ask you to stop what you are doing and roll the stone back in place. Remember what happened the last time the Crystal was exposed to sunlight! The entire population of New Maya City of Worlds disappeared. We have no idea what else the Crystal may be capable of."

"I know you have no idea!" she said with confidence. "I have the full knowledge of a thousand lifetimes. You barely use ten percent of your brain." She reached for another stone that would expose a second shaft of light. Before she could move it Kovax was beside her, his hand on her wrist. "Please," he said. "Why is this so important?"

"The light will be gone soon and I will be unable to complete my task," she said.

"There is always tomorrow," said Kovax. "You can take your request to the Council of Elders and have it properly approved. It is the only safe way."

She moved away from the stone and he released her.

"I know you are goddess of the temple, but I have my duties too," he said.

She looked reticent and reluctant. "Okay. You win." She went over to the first stone she had moved and struggled with it for a moment. She turned, giving both the guards a helpless and coy look. "Please."

Kovax called to the other guard. "Gronk, come give a hand." They placed their staffs of protection against the wall and walked over to her. As they gripped the stone she made a swift move, downing them both before they realized what had happened. She spoke to them as they laid unconscious on the floor. "The Crystal is not my only expertise," she said. "I am also

14

trained in twenty four schools of personal combat."

The light began to fade from the chamber.

"The angle of the sun is changing," she said. "The morning is gone. Am I too late?"

Acting quickly, she dragged the limp bodies beyond the entrance to the chamber. Using her occult knowledge, she pressed her hands and cradled their skulls one at a time.

The will have amnesia when they awaken, she thought. *They will be groggy and the recent past will escape them.* She smiled as she rotated the giant stone door until it fell into place. Like the Crystal, it rested on a pivot point that was easy to move. Using the staffs of protection left behind by the guards, she wedged them between the floor and the door, sealing herself alone inside the chamber.

"Ixpetz! Papaitl!" She examined the room looking for the ghostly images of her past incarnations. There were none to be found. She thought of other past lives, leading up to her present. She had started this lifetime as a man called Cameron Singh, a reincarnated Atlantean who remembered all his past lives. That included the knowledge and life lessons learned throughout thousands of incarnations.

She had inherited all those abilities. The only thing that changed was her gender. "Accursed Crystal," she said. "You set the stage for this. You and my *divine soul*." She spit the words out like they were poison. "If you hadn't opened that higher dimensional place, the Point of Departure or whatever you call it, this never would had happened." She tugged at the dress, anger and loathing clouding her mind and judgment. "The Point of Departure! That's where I met my divine soul. It should have been a spiritual experience. I can think of better outcomes than a sex change operation." She tugged at the dress but it would not come loose. "Well, no more!" she shouted.

"Papaitl. Ixpetz. Pay attention." She called to them even though the ghosts were not there. "I know everything you know about this temple. You are my past, but not for long." She studied the alignment of mirrors, sighting the angles and walking the path that the light would take on its journey from the shaft to the Crystal. The markings on the floor told her where to sit for optimum effect. She settled in, resting in lotus pose.

"Yes, I know everything." She breathed deep. "It's time to prepare. Like you, Papitl, I know the Ritual of Separation. It is not so heinous a task as you imagine. I invite you to watch, or perhaps you would like to perform it with me. Perhaps, like me, you are tired of being manipulated and controlled by our *divine soul*."

Chapter 4

Unacceptable

Guests at The Beachside Bistro in the Eighth Day Village of the Sun were sparse in the afternoon. It was the empty time between lunch and dinner and Philippe, today's host and bartender, busied himself cleaning left over dishes. Monica and Franklin Van Dorn sat at the bar discussing the events of the day. The trip had been disappointing and they didn't see any dolphins, much to Barclay McKenner's dismay.

"Your friend needs you badly," said Monica. "Now more than ever."

Franklin Van Dorn stared into his drink. He had barely touched it over the hour he had been talking to Monica. He looked out of the open sides of the Beachside Bistro towards the Reiki Spa and Resort. Tourists and locals sat in the shade hiding from the bright overhead sun. His eyes kept scanning for his friend.

"Where is he anyway?" asked Van Dorn. "Where is Barclay? He should be here by now."

"He's not coming." She used her psychic skills to verify her first impression, confirming that McKenner was engaged in some other activity. "Don't get off track. I came along on your trip today to observe him. You've asked me for my opinion and I've given it to you. Barclay McKenner is suffering from something like separation anxiety, but it's far more complex than that."

"You said he needs me. What can I do?"

"He won't talk to me directly. And for whatever reason he doesn't want therapy, even though it would help him process the experience."

Philippe turned away from the dirty dishes for a moment.

"Maybe he'll talk to me," he said. "People will often tell their bartender things they won't tell anyone else."

Van Dorn scanned the outside of the bistro again. "Sure! If we can get him to show up." He turned back to Monica. "What would you recommend beside counseling?"

"He needs a better perspective on life," she said. "I'm a Cognitive Behavioral Therapist. One of the principles of CBT has to do with interpretation of events. Human beings naturally try to come up with an explanation for everything that happens to them. You've been out for what, two or three weeks looking for the dolphins and found nothing. Barclay is assuming that he has been rejected by the pod and that they no longer want anything to do with him. That is one explanation. It could be that water temperature made them relocate, or lack of food in the area. Did you notice the fishing fleet close to the reef? That could have something to do with their disappearance. Cognitive Behavioral Therapy encourages you to seek other explanations beyond your initial assessment. It encourages you to seek the truth rather than jumping to conclusions without any evidence."

"So all I have to do is help him find the truth?"

"Well, it's a little more complicated than that."

"You said that already," said Van Dorn. "Please explain. What's complicated about it?"

"I believe that becoming a dolphin was Barclay's dream, a secret fantasy he nurtured after years of swimming and being with them. The Ascension Crystal made it possible. I don't think he was ready to give it up. When he became human again it was almost unbearable for him. You've heard the quips he makes: *Being human is not all it's cracked up to be. Humanity is not the pinnacle of existence. The ocean is like a mother, if only humans could embrace her the way dolphins do.*"

"Yeah, yeah," said Van Dorn. "I've heard him say things like that. So, he wants to be a dolphin again?"

She took a deep breath. "That's only part of it. Obviously he's not happy with humanity. He also assumes the dolphins have rejected him, otherwise he would find the pod and connect

18

with them. This sense of rejection spills over into his assessment of humanity, except in this case he is the one doing the rejecting. This double dose has locked him into a sense of not belonging to either group."

Van Dorn turned and looked towards the door again. "I keep trying to engage him in some kind of activity. I think he's even losing interest in boating and swimming. He's a real downer to be around these days."

"So I see," she said. "Keep in mind he's had a unique experience."

"Not really," interrupted Van Dorn. "He's not the only one who was changed when that damned Ascension Crystal transported everyone to a higher dimension."

"You mean the place called the Point of Departure?"

"Yes," said Van Dorn. "I reviewed the Think Tank report on it. A woman said her husband was now a dog. Another person turned into a giant slug. Can you imagine that? And what about the woman who is now a dinosaur?"

"A dragon," said Monica.

"There's a difference?"

"Of course," said Monica. "Yes, thanks to the Ascension Crystal there are many documented cases of people changing into nonhuman forms, even extinct or fantasy creatures, but Barclay is the first to change back. He offers hope to anyone who has survived such a drastic metamorphosis. But keep this in mind: like your friend Barclay, these changelings may not want to regain their humanity. There may be a good reason why they were transformed. They may even be perfectly happy remaining whatever they have become."

"A giant slug?"

"Whatever," said Monica.

"Cameron Singh is certainly not happy being a woman," said Van Dorn.

19

"I spoke with Kamala Singh after her experience," said Monica, "She is adapting."

"Yes. At least she is human," said Van Dorn. "Barclay should be happy to have two legs and a mouth to speak with."

"I'm not so sure," said Monica. "The dolphins have proven themselves to be spiritual beings. There are some aquatic theme parks around the world where the arenas are now used as classrooms where dolphins teach us about cosmic dimensions and life on Earth. "

"I know. Our dolphin friend Amayatahotep is a part time professor at one of them," said Van Dorn. "He researches dolphin human communication." He took a sip of his drink. "Okay. So there are possible advantages to being a dolphin."

"And Barclay would certainly know what they are. You heard the way he talked about meditation as a dolphin, and that's just one aspect. I've searched the literature and there's nothing like this in any of the psych journals or research papers. There are fantasies where people imagine they have become something. There are even some who dress up and play pretend, but nobody to my knowledge has gone through what he has."

"I'm not so sure," said Van Dorn. "You said you searched the literature, and although I know you meant the published scientific knowledge base, but the answer may actually be found in literature. I'm referring to novels, poems and such. Have you ever read Ovid's *Metamorphoses*?"

"Can't say that I have," said Monica.

"It's an ancient Roman text that contains all kinds of transformation stories."

"I've read it," said Philippe. "The Pantheon of Gods used to regularly change humans and even each other into all kinds of weird things. How do you think the Medusa got a head full of snakes for hair?"

"Yeah," said Van Dorn. "And look at Homer's Odyssey where Circe turned men into pigs."

"That's fantasy. Humans have great imaginations," said Monica. "This is real."

"Yes, but fiction often explores these concepts. There are hundreds of these stories."

"Yes, yes, plenty of transformation stories," she said. "Jekyll and Hyde, werewolves and vampires, weird surgical procedures. There's even a whole superhero genre where characters lead double lives and hide their secret identities. All this is fine but I've been focusing on something more practical and real for my model of his behavior."

Phillipe interrupted their conversation. "I'm going out to the beach for a breath of fresh air," he said. "Help yourselves if you need anything."

Monica didn't let him go without asking, "How's Manny these days? I haven't seen him around."

Manny was the head bartender and a regular feature at the bistro. Philippe smiled at her. "I'm giving him a break. He's infatuated with this woman named Christine. Have you met her?"

"Not yet," said Monica. "But I've heard a lot about her. Do you think she's going to be the next Mrs. Manny Dubois?"

"You're not the first one to suggest that," said Philippe. "Manny will be okay no matter what. It's Barclay McKenner I'm concerned about. I'm glad he's human again. He's a good man. The Village needs him. He's the voice of reason in the Think Tank. A true statesman."

Van Dorn agreed as Philippe turned and left.

"He's a good pilot, too," said Monica, picking up the converstion again.

"He tried to get me to enlist in the Village Flight Corps but I didn't have the time," said Van Dorn.

"What? You don't want to fly one of those crystal airships?" asked Monica.

"You mentioned that you had a model or knew something

that could compare to Barclay's situation. Is it something that might help?"

"I'm not sure," she said. "There's one thing that comes close. Transgendered people often have similar feelings, except in Barclay's case the transition is not a simple sex change."

"You call what happened to Cameron Singh simple?"

"Kamala Singh is a special case," said Monica. "She and I were among the people who helped to debrief and counsel the returning citizens of New Maya City of Worlds after the Ascension Crystal incident. I had a chance to talk to her between sessions. She told me her soul had something to do with transforming her into a woman."

"Her soul?" asked Van Dorn.

"Yes. I wonder if, like Singh, Barclay McKenner's soul had something to do with his transformation. I counseled a lot of people after that event, but I don't recall anybody else mentioning their soul." She suddenly became introspective. "It's a good theory, a starting point. He changed back during meditation. That means something. I wonder what he's really thinking."

"Unless he opens up about it we'll never know."

Monica checke her watch. "I have a shift to cover over at the Village Peace Station. I still work as a Counselor there, even though I'm part of the Think Tank now."

"We all seem to work multiple jobs in the Village," said Van Dorn.

She nodded. "Keep your eye on your friend. There may be a point where he will open up to you. That's when you will be needed the most. Don't say anything. Just listen. Refrain from any comments or offering any solutions. Try not to react to his words. Just listen."

With those simple instructions they parted. Van Dorn watched the evening crowd start to filter in. Philippe returned. He no longer had time for idle chat. Van Dorn got up and wandered outside waiting for the sun to set. He naturally sought solitude as he moved further away from the tourists and the cheerful reverie of the Bistro.

As he passed near the lagoon he heard strange sounds. It was unnerving, something primal and disturbing. Animals roamed wild in the Village sometimes. There was nobody around and he hid behind a tree, peeking out to see what it was. He thought about calling the Peace Station but a feeling in his gut told him to investigate it himself.

"I'm okay," he whispered out loud. "I've swam in the sea alone, been hounded by sharks, even survived a hurricane. This is something simple." Just the same, he bent down and picked up a sizable stick, getting the feel of it as he gently slapped the palm of his hand with it. Summoning his courage, he stepped out from behind the tree.

There was a splash in the water, a disturbance on the surface in the shallows. He heard the wail again, a strange sound that made him freeze in place. He narrowed his eyes and opened his ears but he couldn't make out anything. Holding the stick defensively he slowly advanced towards the sound.

From his angle the sun reflected on the water and distorted his vision. *It looks like a person*, he thought. *But what are they doing here, off the trail and in the riparian zone? Could it be a couple of tourists looking for some privacy?*

Another primal scream made it obvious that it was anything but a tourist. It wasn't even human.

Or was it? As he moved closer he got a glimpse of it. Something floundered in the shallow water of the empty lagoon. It saw him, turning towards Van Dorn, emitting a high pitched shriek unlike anything he had ever heard. He jumped, his nerves grated by the sound in a way that drained him of what little courage he had mustered.

Then he saw who it was. He waded into the water, bending down to assist them.

"Barclay," he said, shaking him like he was a dusty rug. "Barclay, it's me Franklin."

McKenner just stared, then opened his mouth and let out another horrific shriek.

Chapter 5

This Ain't No Horse Race

Randall gently nudged Angi, his beloved giraffe. She responded quickly to his whim, moving from a canter to a full gallop. He hugged her neck, his ear pressed to it, listening to the rhythm of her life. He could hear the blood coursing through her veins, the beat of her heart, the panting of her lungs. He breathed with her, matching her beat, a resonance that lifted both of them out of the realm of the ordinary. It was as if somehow they were one creature.

Cardinal Carmine Jameson on the other hand was having a time of it. The horse he rode was quick enough, but it seemed to have a mind of its own. The jungle was all around and the trail was narrow. He pulled on the reigns, trying to direct Spirit away from the low hanging branches. No luck! It was a constant test of his skill and ability to duck quickly enough to avoid serious injury.

Randall was somewhere up ahead. After a number of challenges, the Cardinal finally caught up with him resting at a peaceful meadow. "I see you wasted no time setting up camp," he said, grateful to finally get off the horse.

There was a large tent, similar to one a Bedouin trader might occupy. Angi grazed nearby, Spirit joining her, one munching on ground cover, the other gnawing at tender treetops. A fire was going, two chairs nearby facing the slowly setting sun.

Randall threw another vegetable on a grill that sat above the flames. "You're right on time," he said. "Dinner's almost done. Have a seat."

Jameson gently rubbed his rear. "No thanks. For now, I prefer to stand." He faced the setting sun. "Ah, God once again draws the curtain on yet another day."

"I'm glad you brought the subject up," said Randall. "I've

been meaning to have a conversation with you."

"About God?" asked Jameson.

"There isn't any subject more important," said Randall. "In my mind, God should be in everyone's daily conversation."

"I agree."

"You have a close connection to the Divine. You're a man of God, aren't you Carmine?"

"Yes," said Jameson. "Of course."

"What do you think God is?"

"I'm not sure I understand the question," said the Cardinal.

"Let me put it another way," said Randall. "When you visualize God, what do you see?"

The Cardinal chuckled.

"What's so funny?" asked Randall.

The Cardinal turned to face him. "Not long ago I visualized God as a friendly old man, a loving father or grandfather who's only concern was my spiritual health and well being."

"I had that vision at one time, too," said Randall.

"So, what do you see when you think of God?" asked the Cardinal.

"I see myself."

Cardinal Jameson again faced the sun. The clouds were gradually changing colors. Deep reds and yellows dominated, cast against a fading blue sky that slowly revealed the stars and planets. "Did you create this beautiful sunset?" He looked towards Randall. "As God, I mean."

"Not personally, of course. You misunderstood me, or maybe I wasn't clear enough. Yes, I am God, albeit one small piece of God. I am a point of light within the mind of God."

"I've read that phrase somewhere." He looked deep in thought for a moment.

"It's from The Great Invocation," said Randall. "I sometimes forget that you are studying all religions." He turned the vegetables in the fire. "Many people cull the world's religions looking for answers. Are you a seeker looking for something?"

"No," said the Cardinal. "Just a student with a strong desire to learn."

"About world religions?"

"Religion is the manifestation of humanity's viewpoint of God. As you said, I am a man of God. What else would I study?"

"A million things," said Randall. "I find God in everything. Physics, astronomy, poetry, medieval history, economics..."

"Economics?" interrupted Jameson.

"Human wants and needs are insatiable," said Randall. "Economics is the science of balancing our resources and getting the most out of them."

"Ah," said the Cardinal. "I can see the other subjects easily. I have been studying the natural sciences and a bit of history as well. Classes at the Eighth Day Village of the Sun are free."

"All knowledge should be free," said Randall.

"Yes! We do agree on this. Education should be free. But there are some things I don't understand. You say you are God. It brings up questions, like: Do you listen to prayers and petitions from yourself? Do you go to a church where you worship yourself? Do you forgive yourself for your sins?"

"That is exactly what I do, exactly how I worship. God is within me. I am grateful for that spark, that guiding light, that piece of the Divine that illuminates the darkness that lies inside myself. My church is in my heart. It is my place of worship. My practice, my service, consists of meditation and yoga. I relax and go into deep states of introspection. It is here that I voice my petitions and prayers. During this time I am connected to my higher self who is my link to God."

"And do you answer your own prayers?"

"Sometimes. More often I find that if I work hard towards my goals I can answer my own prayers."

"Ah, yes," said the Cardinal. "God helps those who help themselves."

"I find that a lot of my prayers are foolish or unnecessary. Even though I feel that I am a part of the Divine Plan, it doesn't always work out as I imagine."

"I have an idea of what you mean. I just never heard it described the way you just described it," said the Cardinal. "My own beliefs are similar. My connection to God is very much internal and personal. In Christianity we speak of the Holy Spirit. It is the Light of the Holy Spirit that helps maintain the connection to God. The big difference is I still visualize God as something external, while to you see Him as internal."

"Him?" corrected Randall. "What makes you so certain that God is male?"

"You have a point," said Jameson. "I have read some texts that express that belief. God could be anything, definitely something beyond our imagination."

"There are as many ways to God as there are people," said Randall.

"You've heard me say that," said Cardinal Jameson. "I once said it to a man who replied, *There is only one way to God and that's through Jesus Christ.* Can the salvation of humanity afford to be so narrow minded?"

"I don't know, your reverence. Obviously for some people, it is." He pulled the vegetables out of the fire. "I think these are done. Would you like to say grace?"

"Why don't you?" The Cardinal looked at Randall with a wide grin. "I'd rather hear it from the mouth of God."

Randall chuckled, about to speak. There was a noise from the jungle, at first a gentle rustle, then the sound of timber cracking. Spirit let out a whinny and Anji snorted, clomping her massive feet on the ground. There was a low growl, deep and threatening.

28

"The animals sense something," said Jameson.

"Yes," said Randall. "Do you sense it too?"

Jameson closed his eyes, focusing his attention on his other senses. He took a breath, an unspoken prayer passing through his mind. In a higher dimension, angels gathered to his side.

Spirit let out a neigh and a wicker.

There was that low growl again. At first it was to his side, and now it was behind him.

Jameson opened his eyes. A wave of fear crashed on his reality. There was a sharp hiss and a raspy growl. The animals grew even more restless. In a low voice he whispered to Randall. "I believe we are being stalked by some kind of jungle cat. Perhaps a jaguar."

"I sense it too."

Jameson looked down at their meal, a roasted pepper, some potatoes and a blackened piece of cauliflower. "Yes!" He drew a deep breath, closing his eyes again. "Whatever it is, I don't think it's a vegetarian."

Chapter 6

I Have No Gills and I Must Breathe

Van Dorn summoned help quickly. Barclay McKenner's eerie squeals and shouts attracted attention while it also sent chills up the spines of all who heard it. Officers Kransky and Roberson of the Village Peace Force arrived shortly, followed by medics, emergency teams, and curious pedestrians. During this time McKenner laid in the shallows of the lagoon, his eyes as blank as a newborn's, his voice as strong as it's cry.

Experts finally decided they could no longer let him flounder in the water. It was getting dark and he needed medical treatment and care. To that end, he was moved via stretcher to an observation room at the village Peace Station where he continued to thrash and wail.

"I've contacted Doctor Rampa," said Peace Chief Wiggins. "I don't know what else we can do."

"Rampa won't be able to help," said Monica. "Barclay McKenner is healthy enough. His body is fine. This is an affliction of the mind."

"Well," said Wiggins. "That's your department." He turned away. "Just the same, have Rampa check him out when he arrives. I'm putting you in charge of this case, Monica. Good luck." He sauntered off towards his office.

Outside an impromptu group calling themselves Friends of Barclay McKenner conducted a prayer vigil, chanting, meditating, and amassing healing energy as they directed it towards the station. Doctor Rampa arrived and they stopped and parted to allow him through.

"Keep up the good work," said the Doctor, turning to face them before entering the building. "Your thoughts and well wishes are not wasted. I have seen many death vigils turn to joy because of things like this."

And so the Friends of Barclay McKenner redoubled their efforts.

Rampa had no difficulty finding his destination. It was not the first time he had been called to the Peace Station to examine someone. He was an auric healer by profession and a curandaro in practice. He had formal training in the medical arts. He held board certifications in many countries and had crossed borders to help humanity in time of need and in time of war. He had seen pandemics, medical anomalies, and countless challenges, but the sight of Barclay McKenner topped it all.

"What are you *seeing*, Doctor?" asked Monica. She said the word with emphasis knowing that it meant something more than visual.

"Dim the lights and I'll tell you," he said. "The aura reveals itself best in the absence of light."

"Yes," said Monica. "Allowing the light within to shine." She had already made her own diagnosis and she anxiously awaited Rampa's. In the relative darkness he saw the problem.

"How long has he been making these strange mewling sounds?" asked Rampa.

"Ever since he was found. I've tried to engage him in conversation. Nothing seems to work."

Barclay let out a piercing scream, looking out at them through one mad, roving eye.

"I know you are psychic," said Rampa. "Do you see what I see?"

"I'm clairsentient," she said. "I feel and sense things, I don't actually *see* them like you do, but I can read auras like you, just differently."

"Then, what do you sense?"

"His energy body is all out of whack," she said. "Normally it follows the general shape of the physical body. Another thing.

There's an odd smell about him. Get close and take a whiff."

Rampa obeyed.

"What is that?" she asked.

"It confirms my diagnosis," said Rampa. "You're right about his energy body. When I look at his aura I don't see the shape of a man. And the smell is unmistakable. It's the smell of salt water and the open sea."

"He was found in the lagoon. Possibly that's where the smell came from. We don't know how long he was laying there in the shallows. According to Franklin Van Dorn it could have been as long as four or five hours."

"Yet he is not wrinkled or dehydrated from the salt water. What do you make of that?"

"OK. Maybe he wasn't in the water that long. We can't be sure."

"Have you felt his skin?"

"Yes," said Monica. "I wanted to try some massage. He reacted violently to my touch. I gently tried to pet him but he jerked away. His skin felt unnatural, like something I can't describe."

"Yes. Either way, Barclay McKenner is far from human anymore. More like something in between."

"What do you mean?"

"His aura is unmistakable. It's in the shape of a dolphin. In some strange way, I would say he has become a dolphin trapped in the body of a human."

Chapter 7

Ocelot of Information

"What should we do?" asked Jameson. The growling continued at regular intervals, the rustle of leaves and the sound of wood cracking. It was a chorus of anxiety.

Randall noticed the Cardinal's agitation. "Be still for a moment."

"What about the animals?"

"Anji will protect Spirit. Giraffes have huge hooves. Even a lion won't attack a giraffe, they know better. Anji could easily stomp a jungle cat to death."

"Good," said the Cardinal. "Now what about us?"

"We keep the fire going," said Randall. "Make it bigger. Wild beasts will not come close to the flames."

There was another growl. This time from a different direction. "It's circling us," said Jameson.

"Not exactly," said Randall. "Close your eyes. Don't you sense it? It's prowling in a semicircle and avoiding the animals. It appears to be more interested in us."

Jameson closed his eyes. He swore he could hear heavy breathing close and to his right. He thought, *It is not my destiny to be eaten by a jaguar.*

No, it is not, came an answer. He reacted. Whether in his ear or in his head, he still heard it, as if someone had clearly said it.

There was another low growl, this time from behind him. The hairs on the back of his neck raised, sending a tingling sensation down his spine.

The voice came again. *Perhaps not a jaguar. Perhaps it is your destiny to be eaten by an ocelot.*

Despite his ability to remain still and calm, Jameson shuddered, an involuntary gesture his body demanded. He opened his eyes and looked at the fire, thinking it may not be big enough. He reached for some kindling, ready to put it on the flames.

That is not the fire you should be stoking. Try the Violet Flame instead.

Jameson dropped the kindling. "Eh? Who's saying that?"

"Did you hear something?" asked Randall. He took a breath and slipped into a deep state of awareness, activating his own psychic senses.

There was another growl. Jameson swore he could feel hot breath on his neck.

Randall was staring over the Cardinal's shoulder. "Yes. I hear it growling too," he said. "Don't be alarmed. Don't make any sudden moves, but I think it came from that creature behind you."

The Cardinal turned his head slowly, catching a glimpse of the animal. It was close enough to pounce. It looked like an over-sized house cat with strange markings. The eyes were outlined in white, the ears slightly larger and rounded, shaped more like a rat's. The body had leopard like markings that ran together, something between spots and mottled stripes. He turned back towards Randall and whispered, "So, he won't come near the flames, you say?"

Randall smiled showing no fear. His psychic senses alerted him that there was nothing to fear. He was one with nature, one with the cat. They were part of the same fabric of energy that made up God, the Universe, and everything in existence. And what creature, knowing this, would harm itself? "Welcome, my friend," he said.

To his surprise, the creature answered him. "Thank you. I saw your fire. I am Tlacoocelotl."

"Eh?" Cardinal Jameson turned around to face the cat. "What is this? You are the one who has been speaking to me?"

"You didn't hear him before?" asked Randall. He looked at Tlacoocelotl. "You really weren't going to eat him, were you?"

Tlacoocelotl scanned the Cardinal. "Nah. Too scrawny. His bones would get stuck in my teeth."

Jameson looked nervously relieved, unsure of the comment or exactly what was happening. He said a silent prayer and felt better. He could sense the presence of the angels around him, especially his guardian angel. "This is strange. How is it that an animal can talk?"

"You're an animal and you can talk," said Tlacoocelotl.

"Stop messing with Cardinal Jameson," said Randall. "He's my friend."

"I know who he is. I like to test people and judge the level of fear in them," said Tlacoocelotl. He turned towards the Cardinal. "It's okay. You didn't run from me."

"Am I going crazy or is this animal talking?" asked the Cardinal.

"It's your psychic gifts, Carmine," said Randall. "They have been activated. I see it in your aura."

"Is this how psychic things work? It makes me imagine things?"

"I hear him too. What are the odds that we both hear the same thing?"

"You are not imagining things," said Tlacoocelotl. "Just sensing things in a higher dimension. The world of solid flesh is very dense and of course it keeps you focused here. For some people, physical reality is all there is, all they will ever know."

The Cardinal nodded. "I see." He began to feel more at ease with the strange circumstances. He had seen many odd things recently. This seemed to be another one of them. Just a normal conversation.

With a... what? Higher dimensional jungle cat? he thought.

"Cameron Singh told me all about you," said Tlacoocelotl. "You are the holy man who seeks all knowledge."

"Ah, so you know Singh," said Randall. "Then you know what happened to her."

"Yes, and I also know what she is trying to do, which is why I sought you out and why I am here. I need your help. Both of you."

"You need our help?" asked Jameson. "Just what can we do for you, eh? Especially here, in the middle of the jungle at night. We haven't even had our dinner."

The ocelot growled, saliva dripping out of its mouth. "And neither have I."

"The Cardinal is right," said Randall. "It's dark out. What do you want?"

"I will guide you," said Tlacoocelotl. "I am a spirit guide. Do you not recognize that? Do you not trust me?"

"What's the big rush?" asked Cardinal Jameson. "Where do you want to guide us?"

"To New Maya City of Worlds," said Tlacoocelotl.

"We are headed there too," said Randall. "We'll be there tomorrow."

"Tomorrow will be too late," said the ocelot. "Kamala Singh is about to do something dangerous and soul shattering. Nobody in the temple will take me seriously. She has many blind followers and empty headed clergy that gather around her. The same way jungle vines surround a tree, they hide her from the world. They exist to build her ego and do her bidding. If she is allowed to carry out her will, the newly built Temple of the Ascension Crystal could collapse. The whole city of New Maya and everyone within it may disappear, just as they did so recently. And this time they may never return."

"How do you know these things?" asked Randall.

"I am a relic of our past," said Tlacoocelotl. "A sacred temple cat charged with protecting the secrets of our holy places. I taught Cameron Singh about the Temple of the Sacred Jaguar when he found his way to me during a storm. I am an ancient creature. I have taught other incarnations of him."

"Her," corrected Randall.

The ocelot growled. "In one lifetime he was a high priest called Papitl. I taught Papitl and then his son, Ixpetz. There were others as well. Now these spirits of the past seek your help. I seek your help. We are bound by duty to the Ascension Crystal and must protect its interests."

Two ghosts materialized beside the giant cat. "Listen to Tlacoocelotl," said Ixpetz. "Have some compassion for your friend who needs you."

Cardinal Jameson saw something, an orb of light or something. Was it speaking to him? "I'm not so sure," said the Cardinal. He looked towards Randall. "What is going on here?"

"I'm not so sure myself," said Randall.

"It's as plain as anything," said Tlacoocelotl. "You hear our plea. Kamala Singh and the whole City of New Maya is in danger. We need your help. What is your answer?"

"Yes," said Ixpetz. "Will you help us?"

"I've been tricked by lower astral beings before," said Randall.

"I am Papaitl. I was once a priest of the Temple. What Kamala Singh is about to do is a sacrilege. We cannot stop her alone. Must we keep asking?"

"If we can see and hear you like this, why aren't you talking to her?" asked the Cardinal.

"We tried to stop her," said Papaitl. "We failed. We hope you can do better. She is your friend, after all."

Ixpetz faced the jungle cat. "They need convincing."

"Yes," said Tlacoocelotl.

"Perhaps the Violet Flame will help them understand." said Papaitl.

"How do you know about that?" asked the Cardinal. "What do you know about the Violet Flame?"

"Everything." Tlacoocelotl leaned in close to the Cardinal, his voice changing. Carmine Jameson recognized it, the sound of his old friend Father Kaupon. It was he who taught him about the Violet Flame of Saint Germain. "Now do as I say. Stare into the fire, Carmine. Bring out the color violet, the sacred ray that brings forth the higher self, the intellect of the soul. There are times when the soul must be the warrior. This is one of them." As he softly said the words the Cardinal was lulled into a deep meditative state while staring at the fire.

Papaitl whispered similar words into Randall's ear. Together the corporeal bridged the gap between physical and spiritual. The flame grew quiet, the red and yellow colors disappearing from the glowing embers, traveling up to the tips of the fire until it was entirely blue. As the Cardinal concentrated, this slowly diffused into a deep indigo-violet flame. His lips uttered a prayer and the flame became still and stable, no longer a simple fire. By his will and his focus it had been converted into a divine object. It glowed in a higher dimension, and it was by this method that he further awakened his higher senses. By focusing on the indigo flame and its color, he and everything around him was raised to this higher level of vibration.

"Listen to me now," said Tlacoocelotl, still in the voice of Father Kaupon. "I will explain to you what she is trying to do. The Ascension Crystal can be used for many things. Healing, teleportation, communication beyond life, even contacting beings in other dimensions and in other galaxies. You already know how it can open the doorway to the Point of Departure. In that place life issues and spirit communication blend into a tangible experience. One of the other things the Crystal can do is connect a person with their soul, strong enough that they can meet face to face. Imagine that! But like a pendulum that can swing both ways, it is also capable of opposite. In this sense, it can also be used to sever that connection. And that is what Kamala Singh wishes to do."

The flame faltered.

"Sever her connection to her soul?" said Jameson. "How is that possible?"

"It is possible," said Tlacoocelotl, now in his own voice.

"What will happen when she does that?" asked Randall.

"That is something we don't exactly know," said Ixpetz.

"It is the first light of dawn that we fear," said Papaitl. "It will activate the Crystal. She has already set the path that the light will follow through the temple to find its way to the Crystal. The dark corridors with their mirrors and colored lenses have been turned and are ready. The light of the early morning will activate the energy and trigger this counter purpose."

"The Crystal will not react favorably to being used like that," said Tlacoocelotl. "It has a life of its own, a life beyond the physical reality you perceive. It has power you cannot fathom. It has been considering the collapse of the temple as an option, a way to bury itself and hide once again from humanity. This would be a great loss as the Crystal can help evolve your species. Knowledge and history are at stake. Are these not also reasons to move quickly?"

"Think also of the City and it's inhabitants," said Ixpetz. "You have the power to protect them."

Randall looked over at the Cardinal for confirmation. Jameson nodded in agreement. "Singh needs my help, and a divine soul is at risk, let alone the souls of everyone in New Maya. How can I refuse? I am in the business of saving souls."

"Well." said Randall. "That's final then. Let's eat our vegetables and be on our way."

Chapter 8

Locked Into a Decision

Kamala Singh was distracted. She heard a voice from the other side of the heavy door that was jammed shut.

"Mistress, the entrance is blocked. Are you okay?"

She recognized Tubork. He had recovered quicker than she imagined. "I'm fine," she said.

"The priests and servants are concerned. They asked us to check on you."

"Please! I'm fine," said Singh.

"We are trying to open the door but it seems to be stuck."

"Don't worry about it," she said. "I will use the Crystal in the morning to open the door. I only need the sunlight to activate it. Go back to your normal duties."

"We will stand guard here, Priestess. You need only call us if you need us."

It was an acceptable outcome. The sunlight would be here soon. *The guards will keep any meddlers away and give me time for the ritual*, she thought. Kamala Singh smiled, summoning her best voice. "Thank you, my loyal protectors. I feel safer already."

Chapter 9

The Guiding Spirit

Tlacoocelotl moved through the jungle with grace, the humans less assuredly. Randall and the Cardinal tagged behind, clumsily avoiding low hanging branches, roots and rocks along the trail.

"I still don't understand why we couldn't take the animals," said the Cardinal. "As uncomfortable as it was, I would prefer the saddle to this."

"You heard the ocelot," said Randall. "Ixpetz and Papaitl are going to take care of Anji and Spirit. We rode them all day and they need rest."

"And we don't?"

"Are you tired?" asked Randall.

"Not really."

"It might have something to do with the leaves of the tree Tlacoocelotl told us us eat."

The Cardinal nodded. "Yes. Perhaps you're right. Still, I would have enjoyed settling in for the sunset and some more interesting conversation. I still don't understand all this."

"It seems to be some kind of convergence of forces or energy," said Randall. "Mystical, higher dimensional beings are involved here. Something larger than life is happening. We are Singh's best friends. You are a priest, a trained and ordained savior of souls. You have experienced firsthand what the Crystal can do. Who better to recruit for this mission? "

"Okay," said the Cardinal. He tripped over a rock, catching himself as he barely avoided a fall.

Randall stopped and steadied him for a moment. "Even

though the moon is up I still have trouble seeing where I'm going."

"I know, and what's the big hurry? Hey, Mr. Ocelot," shouted the Cardinal. "How about slowing down a bit?"

Tlacoocelotl appeared behind them. "I forget you only have two legs while I have four." He shook his head sadly. "Not very efficient."

"Ah," said the Cardinal. "For some kind of higher dimensional spiritual being you have a lot of low opinions of us."

"It's the opinion of a lot of higher dimensional spiritual beings," said Tlacoocelotl.

The Cardinal sneered.

"It's all right," said the Ocelot. "I believe in you and your kind, otherwise I would not be here. You will achieve your potential." The cat looked away before adding, "Some day."

"Are you okay Carmine?" asked Randall, still supporting his friend.

"How much farther is it?" asked the Cardinal.

"We are over half way there," said Tlacoocelotl. "This trail is far quicker than the other one you were following. We must be there before the sun rises." He studied the sky. "It may already be too late. Let's keep moving."

"Okay, but a little slower perhaps, eh?" said the Cardinal.

And so they began again, following what was little more than a game trail. Occasionally Tlacoocelotl would screech and growl clearing the path of any unwanted predators as he made the way safe for the humans behind him. At a slightly slower pace, Randall and the Cardinal passed the time talking. In doing so they drew their focus away from their fatigue.

"I've been thinking about this idea that you are God," said Jameson. "So, where does this leave the Holy Church?"

"Churches are still needed. They are bastions of morality. They help the faithful understand and draw closer to God. They establish a spiritual minded community of souls wherever they are built. And my path is no different. It's just that I seek God within myself and not inside a building."

"I have felt that connection too." Jameson pointed to his heart. "Right here."

"Ah, yes," said Randall. "And that's where my church is. That's where I worship."

"The IRS defines a church as having literature, a place of worship, and holding services. It doesn't get any simpler than that," said the Cardinal. "I see you only have two out of three."

Randall laughed. "My church has no collection plate and so I don't need the tax deduction. As far as my literature, it is written in my heart daily with every deed and with every action that I consecrate to God and to my higher purpose."

Jameson nodded. "In my belief, a church is the house of God."

"As is my heart," said Randall. "Whether you meditate or worship in a church, the path to God remains an inward one. It is up to us to forge our relationship with the Divine."

"You asked me earlier about my concept of God," said Cardinal Jameson. "I've had some time to think about it."

"Yes," said Randall. "And what did you come up with?"

"As I said before: like you, I feel God in my heart. Through me, I do His works."

"You use a male pronoun again," said Randall. "Do I detect a little of that old man in the sky imagery?"

The Cardinal chuckled. "Maybe. I prefer to think of the old man as an early concept of God, a foundation I could build upon. For now I will stick to the male pronoun as I prefer the image of a loving Father."

"Yes, I see," said Randall. "I believe God is genderless, more all encompassing, both a paternal father and a divine mother. The yin and the yang. So, explain to me, how do you see God now?"

"I see God in everything," said Jameson. "I see Him when I look out at the night sky, when I peer into the matrix of a sunflower, when I watch the sea lapping against a shoreline, vying for control of the land. And I don't just see Him. I hear Him in a baby's laugh or the soft sigh of a breeze. I touch His face when I pray and meditate in silence. I taste his sweetness in bread and wine. I feel his presence in the warmth of the sun."

Their imagination lingered for a while before Randall said, "Well put, my friend."

"I just wish people would be more tolerant of each other's beliefs," said the Cardinal. "So many wars have been fought over the ideology of religion. So many faiths have defined themselves as the one true religion and the only path to salvation."

"We all have our idea of what God is," said Randall. "It's hard looking up into the higher dimensions. It's easier to look down where you see things clearly in three or four states of matter."

"Is that how this psychic thing works?" asked the Cardinal. "Am I actually seeing things in a higher dimension? Am I talking to invisible beings?"

"What makes you think you aren't? An experience is real, whether it occurs in your head or in the three dimensional world."

"Yes," said the Cardinal. "Every mental patient I ever met believes the same thing."

Randall gave him a sideways glance. "Many people talk to invisible beings," he said. "They just won't admit it publicly. It brands then as crazy."

"So am I psychic or crazy?"

"Yes," answered Randall.

He was grinning when Jameson looked over at him, and the Cardinal had to laugh as well.

"I'm not sure I understand it myself," said Randall. "I prefer to think of myself as intuitive and not psychic. There's a difference."

"Really? Explain it."

"Psychic includes all kinds of things, maybe even what you're experiencing now. It's an external thing, you see. Communicating with other beings, past life regressions, seances, card readings, that sort of thing. Intuitive comes from knowing, from trusting some inner instinct that guides our lives and all the decisions we face."

"What you're taking about is surrendering to the will of God."

"On my path I call it dissolving the ego," said Randall. "It's the only thing that stands between me and clear communication with God."

"Some people ignore God altogether," said the Cardinal. "In my concept of God, my soul is like an intermediary, something that is closer to the Divine than I could ever be. This soul is our own, our refuge in times of strife, the rock in stormy waters. I imagine my soul understands things about God that I will never see from my Earthly perspective."

Randall nodded. "Sometimes in conversations with my soul I pass on all the frustrations I have, all the worry I carry, and all the struggle with the world of humans. My soul consumes it like a buffet for a starving man."

"Heaven on Earth could be found, if only we all lived like the Children of God," said the Cardinal.

"Yes," said Randall.

"That's not original," said Jameson. "I heard it somewhere."

"I have been hearing you two jabber away," interrupted Tlacoocelotl. The sacred animal appeared behind them matching their easy pace.

"Eh?" said Jameson turning. "And do you have something to add?"

"Maybe," he said. "Do you want to hear it?"

"Of course. We're listening."

"Each of you has free will and, depending on how much you bend your will, some degree of control over your life. It doesn't matter whether that control is coming from your earthly ego or from your spiritual soul, or even some hybrid of the two that you imagine yourself to be. From all I have seen in my long lifetime as a spirit guide, I have noticed that despite their level of spirituality, humans can still lose control and, in the process, lose themselves. To maintain control you must know yourself and conquer the banal, the beast that thrives within. You must keep open the connection you share to God. Be true to yourself and to your image of God, whatever that may be, but above all know yourself. If you are unsure of that, trust your soul and let it be your guide and warrior."

"Good advice from an animal," said the Cardinal.

Tlacoocelotl sneered. "And you are not an animal?"

"What about evil?" asked Randall. "Do you have something to say about that?"

"Evil cannot be conquered in the world, only resisted from within," said Tlacoocelotl.

"I've heard that before too. It's not original," said the Cardinal.

Tlacoocelotl let our a low growl. "Ah, yes. And of course everything you say is original."

The cardinal nodded.

"There is much I could teach you both, but we have reached our destination." The narrow path suddenly opened into a meadow. Across the lawn in the moonlight they could see the outline of the Temple of the Ascension Crystal. As they emerged they saw their animals, Anji and Spirit, grazing to the side.

"How did they get here?"

"I told you that Ixpetz and Papitl would take care of them," said Tlacoocelotl..

"But how?" said the Cardinal. "Please explain."

"There are dimensional portals that connect places on the Earth. They simply led them through the portal."

"So?" said the Cardinal. "Why didn't we take the portal? Why did you make us walk, eh?"

"Silly, the portal they used is for animal only. No humans allowed."

"Ah, again with the restrictions and judgments." said the Cardinal.

"Not my rules," said the sacred ocelot. "At one time humans had all this knowledge and more. Telepathy, psychic gifts, and the ability to easily manifest your needs. These were lost when humans fell from grace. But it's okay. In your cleverness you have replaced telepathy with telephones, your psychic gifts with analytical computers and your ability to manifest with ordering things off the internet. And all you need is money!"

"We don't use money in the village," said Randall. "Only when dealing with the outside world."

"OK. So you call them tokens instead of coins. We'll see how that experiment goes," said Tlacoocelotl. "Come now, daylight approaches soon."

They arrived at the temple door to find guards there. "No one is to enter," said the taller of the two. "The temple is closed now."

Randall looked toward the ocelot. "They cannot see me," said Tlacoocelotl. "You're on your own, but you must gain entrance."

"You have to let us in," said Randall. "We have an audience with our friend Kamala Singh. She awaits our presence."

"The Priestess is the reason the temple is sealed. It cannot be opened without her approval."

Ixpetz and Papaitl walked out of the wall of the temple, their ghostly forms becoming visible only to Randall, Tlacoocelotl and the Cardinal.

"We must get in," said Papaitl. "She has locked herself in the Ascension Chamber and awaits the sunlight."

"It comes quickly," said Ixpetz, studying the sky. The stars were already beginning to disappear, the planets still maintaining their hold against the dawn.

The Cardinal turned to Randall. "What do we do now?"

"We wait," said Randall.

"No," said Tlacoocelotl. "Soon it will be too late. The time is now."

"Can you overpower the guards?" asked Ixpetz.

Before Randall could answer, one of the guards said. "You could go to the New Maya Council of Elders. They are the ruling authority. Besides the High Priestess Kamala, they are the only ones who can unlock the temple. The Crystal must be protected and controlled."

"And it is in control of a madwoman now," said Ixpetz.

Randall looked at the Cardinal. "I know the people on the Council. I will go to them and plead our case."

"It will be too late," said Papaitl. "Don't you understand?"

Randall wasn't listening. He turned towards Cardinal Jameson. "You stay here, my friend. I sense something may happen and you may be able to somehow gain access to the temple."

"A psychic premonition?"

"This is more intuitive."

"All right," said the Cardinal. "I just wish I had a place to sit. A chair would be nice."

"There's one at the top of the temple," said the smaller guard. "Just follow the steps. It's a great place to watch the sun rise."

Tlacoocelotl winced, then sprung into action. "Let's be at it then. Quickly! I have an idea." The ocelot led him to a staircase built on the outside of the temple. He and the Cardinal began the arduous journey up the steps while Randall walked off toward the core of buildings that were part of New Maya City of Worlds.

The steps were narrow. Progress was slow for the Cardinal. Tlacoocelotl pounced easily from step to step, sometimes leaping with amazing agility across many of them at a time. "Hurry," he would say, trying to be encouraging.

The Cardinal had to catch his breath. His chest heaved like a sail luffing in a strong wind. Tlacoocelotl appeared behind him. "Stop doing that," said the Cardinal as he caught his breath. "You startle me."

"If I could carry you on my back I would," said Tlacoocelotl. He looked toward the sky. They were barely half way up the stone steps of the pyramid. The dawn began to shine on the other side of the temple. A long shadow formed on the open lawn behind them as the sun broke the horizon.

Ixpetz appeared beside Tlacoocelotl. "It is of no matter now. We are too late."

Chapter 10

The Power of Light

Kamala Singh sat in silent meditation, the culmination of a ritual she had been practicing all night. She sat at just the right spot, at the right angle, facing the Crystal while she waited for it to activate.

Sunlight streamed into the Ascension Chamber, a tight beam focused like a laser by mirrors and lenses of ancient design. It struck the Crystal and lit it up. The giant Crystal glowed, emitting bands of colored light in all directions. It reflected off of images and words embedded in the stone walls of the room. Imperfections and designs in the rock made the light split into more and more wavelengths. Colors were everywhere, merging into regions of intense white light and forming areas of shadows. Vortexes of energy formed, swirling with colors, lines of intention, and pools of darkness.

"Yes," said Kamala. "I can feel it. Give me what I desire. Free me from the control of my immortal soul."

There was a flash and she gasped for breath, hyperventilating until dizziness overcame her. Her eyelids fluttered. The chamber continued to resonate with color and shadows of darkness that passed over the priestess. There was a high pitched whistle, sounding like the winds of change blowing in a hurricane.

The Crystal shuddered, sending out a wave of energy. It spread like a tsunami, not only outward but upward and into the higher dimensions, wreaking havoc as it tore through the unseen cosmos.

With that, Kamala Singh collapsed forward and lost consciousness, coming to rest silently on the stone floor.

Chapter 11

The New Maya Council of Missing Elders

Randall easily found the meeting hall of the New Maya Council of Elders. He had been there before many times as both a guest and a speaker. There were deep ties between the sister cities as both New Maya City of Worlds and the Eighth Day Village of the Sun sought a higher purpose to their existence. Trade between the two combined with a steady stream of outside visitors supplied them both with an excess of money. Dealings with the world in general were often calculated as a loss. The citizens had no use for money in a community where productivity was high and most everything was free. This was only possible in a spiritual society where there was no avarice, greed or need to accumulate riches and material things. Here the darkness of the human heart was uncovered and illuminated by the Light of God, no matter what form the Supreme Deity assumed.

The sun was barely up and the paths through the City of Worlds were well lit. With every gain in sunlight more streetlights went dark, a reminder that time was running out. It was early morning and the council building appeared empty. The door was open and the lights inside the meeting hall remained bright and inviting. An old man sat at the other end of the room near the raised dais that supported the chairs and tables usually occupied by the council members. A bird was perched on the back of one of the beautifully crafted seats. Near the old man a goat munched on some grass piled up in the corner.

The old man heard the footsteps. He was blind, but you would not think it so. His awareness was keen and his senses honed to a new level of compensation. Somehow he could not only feel the presence of somebody but also see into the depths of them and know things that even they may hide from themselves. Like Tiresias, the cursed seer of ancient Greece, it was a two edged gift.

"Who's there?" he asked sniffing the air. "Ah, never mind, I would know your scent anywhere, Baba Randall."

"Yes, Elder Bruce. I recognize you." He noticed the signs of aging, the weariness in Bruce's now empty eyes.

"Good to see you, Randall of the Village. Come! Sit beside me."

"Am I early? Where is the rest of the council?"

"Gone. Missing. Somewhere beyond. We are all that remain."

Randall scanned the room seeing only Bruce and the animals. "We?"

"Yes," said Elder Bruce. "As you know we experienced a strange event when the Ascension Crystal was unearthed by Dr. Candle. You may recall that he was one of the archaeologists working on the temple project."

"Yes," said Randall. "The Crystal caused everyone in New Maya City of Worlds to disappear. Our communities routinely monitor each other's cameras. We noticed the city was empty, so we sent an expedition to investigate."

"You did!" said Elder Bruce. "Without your help we would have all vanished forever, lost somewhere in a higher dimensional place called the Point of Departure. Somehow you freed us and some of us were returned to this world, not all in human form. Modified, as I like to say."

There was a fire and a puff of smoke as the bird perched on the chair burst into flames. Randall turned, not sure of what he saw.

"It's okay, she'll be back," said Elder Bruce. "That was Councilwoman Perry. As you know, when we were released from the control of the Crystal we returned, but as I said not everyone was human. For example," he nodded towards the now empty chair. "Perry became a phoenix, something that never before existed in this reality. She goes through this cycle of flaming death and rebirth about once a week." He looked off and remarked, "I wonder if it is painful, burning up like that."

The goat stopped eating and raised its head, braying from the corner.

"Ah, yes. And this is Diana Gray, our council recorder and secretary. She is now a male goat with few interests other than eating."

Randall's heart sank. Elder Bruce felt it. "What's the matter?" he asked.

"I came here because I need your help," said Randall. "I need the help of the Council."

"And here I thought you had come to help us."

"Not this time, I'm afraid," said Randall. "It's something more urgent. But I promise to send help. I will return and see what I can do."

"Then, what do you need? What can we do for you?"

"Where is the rest of the Council?" asked Randall.

"You mean besides an old blind man and these odd creatures?" said Bruce. "Gone. They never returned." He drew a deep breath. "Some of us moved on. Not just some, nearly a third or more of the population of New Maya City of Worlds never returned. This higher dimensional place was not called the Point of Departure by accident. You were not there, Randall, but the draw of it is strong. It is a place where existence can be contemplated and molded into whatever shapes we can imagine. Life problems can be considered and understood. I wanted to stay there, to work out a few things and move on with the rest, but it wasn't to happen. So here I am. Of those that materialized only two thirds retained their human form. The rest became all manner of creatures, mythical or otherwise. Some, I suspect, even became trees and plants. I swear I have had conversations with vegetables, although it may be dementia setting in. This whole affair is wrapped around my brain like an angry boa constrictor, and it won't let go." He became agitated, the anxiety and the inner pressure of his experience building again as he recalled it.

"Still, I need the help of the Council," said Randall.

"Haven't you been listening to me? I am the Council." He calmed his voice. "What do you need, Randall?"

"Permission to enter the Temple of the Ascension Crystal."

"Whatever for? That place is cursed, Kamala Singh has seen to that. You don't need my permission to go there, you need hers."

"Can you at least give me a writ allowing me access. The guards said the Council could grant it."

"If you think it would help. If you need it..." Elder Bruce turned towards the goat. "Diana, can you draw that up for us?"

Randall half expected the animal to do what Elder Bruce asked, but it did not happen. She, or he, continued to munch on dead grass and leaves, not even stopping to answer him.

Bruce turned towards Randall and laughed. "Sorry. It's my little joke, a vain attempt to follow decorum. Of course, I'll do it. Find me a piece of paper and write whatever you want on it. Then I will sign it and stamp it with the Council seal."

Chapter 12

Not Again!

Although they were never built as attractions, the more interesting places frequented by tourists and locals alike were the Eighth Day Village of the Sun sex fountains. A smattering of these private vestibules were scattered throughout the Village. Today this particular one was shared between Manny and Christine. At the head of the trail that led to it, the "occupied" sign was conspicuously displayed. As an extra measure Manny had closed the secure gate blocking the entrance. On the Village computer system it now appeared as occupied and closed.

This sex fountain was integrated into a natural waterfall that cascaded down the face of the Crystal Mountain. In addition to the play area there was a lounge with a view that looked off into the deep blue Pacific. Manny and Christine were on break enjoying the scene while listening to the gentle flow of water in the background. The morning sun was slowly rising, casting the shadow of the mountain across the sea. The refraction of light created an aura around the shadow giving it an appearance unlike anything else on Earth. The motion of the sea and the waves only added to the effect.

"How many women have you taken here?" asked Christine.

"Are you serious?" he said. "I told you. This is the first time I've been to this place."

"Then how did you know the way to get here?"

"I just asked the Village computer for directions."

"Oh, right," she said. "It was quite a hike to get here, but well worth it."

"I heard about this fountain at the Beachside Bistro. Randall told me he used it now and then, but it was no fun with less than thirty people."

Christine chuckled. "It's certainly big enough for it."

"The tourists that find their way here rave about it. As a bartender I hear about a lot of interesting things and this is one place I always wanted to check out. I just had to find the right partner." He took her hand and raised it to his lips, giving it a gentle kiss.

She reclined in his arms, the warmth of his body flowing out from his heart and into her, bathing her in love as easily as the water had so recently streamed across her naked form. Under the falling water they had practiced their art, an embrace as old as human creation, a joining of souls eager to explore the landscapes of love.

He reached over and kissed her, whispering quiet things in her ear, professing his love as he gently nibbled on her lobes.

There was a noise nearby, a muffled beep, steady and persistent.

She withdrew from his arms. "I know that sound."

He advanced toward her a bit. "So do I. But that's no reason to stop what we are doing."

She wiggled free from him, slipping to the other side of the sofa. The beep continued. "Well, are you going to answer it? You're a member of the Eighth Day Village of the Sun Think Tank, the highest authority. Don't you think it might be something important?"

"Not as important as you," he said.

She huffed, stood up and went to the wall where his pants hung on a hook. She took the communicator out of the pocket and pressed the respond button. "Hello. This is Christine, Mr. Dubois' secretary. How may I help you today?"

Randall chuckled on the other end. "Good to hear from you, Christine. Thank you for answering my call. Can you relay a message to Mr. Dubois for me?"

Manny got up and moved behind her. He wrapped his arms around her waist squeezing her in a gentle hug. "He's here with me now," she said. "Go ahead." She moved the communicator away from her ear so they could both hear.

"Tell Manny I need him. I know you are both busy and signed out for the day. I tried to assign this mission to Barclay McKenner but he is incapacitated at the moment."

"Incapacitated?" asked Manny.

"Unable to fly," said Randall. "That's why I need you. You're the only available pilot."

"What about Nash?"

"He's in Africa with Mel Ewing. I'm sorry to interrupt your vacation with Christine but it's very important."

Manny whispered to Christine. "It always is."

Randall heard it and said nothing.

"What is it this time?" asked Manny.

"I need you to go to the airport and pick up Dr. Barnheart and the Gorgofsky twins. Take a crystal ship and bring them to New Maya City of Worlds as quickly as you can."

"What's the emergency?" asked Manny. "Is it the Ascension Crystal again?"

"Yes," he answered. "Kamala Singh is going to use it to sever the connection to her soul. The Council of Elders is concerned about what the Ascension Crystal could do. We need your help. As a particle physicist, you can offer a scientific approach to the problem. You also experienced firsthand what the Crystal can do. I have Barnheart and the Gorgofsky twins in transit. How soon can you meet them?"

"We're not far from the Crystal Mountain tram station. We can be at the airport within the hour."

"We?" whispered Christine.

He gently kissed her on the neck. "I thought you loved to fly

57

in a crystal airship," he whispered.

"I do," she said.

Randall knew exactly where they were. He heard the waterfall in the background. The whispered comments and wet kisses were easily amplified by the communicator. Of course, it helped that he pressed the call location button on his end. "Please, Manny," he said, letting out a sigh that betrayed his tension. "You have no idea what's at stake here. It's more than the soul of our friend, more than you can imagine. Please! Pick up Barnheart and the twins and get here as soon as you can."

Chapter 13

Overcoming Your Fears

"You're too late," said Ixpetz. "Kamala Singh has activated the Crystal. She is locked in the Ascension Chamber and there's nothing we can do now."

The Cardinal stopped climbing the steep stairs that led to the top of the temple pyramid. He turned around, about to descend to the bottom when Papaitl appeared in front of him. "She's unconscious," said the ghost. "The Crystal has done its work. She is little more than a golem now, empty of soul and spirit. She is beyond our help."

"You give up too easily," said Tlacoocelotl. "There is one last chance. Come on." He signaled the Cardinal to follow him as he leaped, moving sideways across the pyramid and off the stairs. There were wide, flat ledges that went around the temple. Jameson followed the sacred cat around two corners and onto the brightly lit side of the temple that faced the rising sun. "Over here," yelled the ocelot.

There was a square hole in the wall beside the ledge. Tlacoocelotl stood before it pointing like a dog on the hunt.

"What?" asked the Cardinal. "What's down there?"

"This tunnel carries the light that flows into the Ascension Chamber."

"Good idea," said the Cardinal. "I'll find something to block it."

Ixpetz was beside him. "It's too late," he said. "The light has already activated the Crystal."

"He has a better idea," said Papaitl.

Jameson could only respond by saying, "Eh?"

59

"Yes," said Tlacoocelotl.

"He wants you to crawl down there."

"Down there?" said Jameson. The tunnel was dark. He reached in with his hand and felt the walls. Mud, thick and ugly, was all over his arm when he retracted it. "Are you mad? It's dark and I can't see where I'm going."

"The light will be behind you most of the way," said Tlacoocelotl.

"We will guide you," said Ixpetz.

The Cardinal sized it up. "I don't know if I can fit in there. I'll probably get stuck."

"No you won't," said Papaitl. "Trust us."

"There must be another way," said the Cardinal. "Randall will be back shortly with the Council. The guards will let us pass."

He started to turn away and go back to the stairs when Tlacoocelotl blocked the ledge. "Would it not be better to endure a little dirt and save your friend's immortal soul?"

"Singh needs you," pleaded Ixpetz.

"We need you," said Papaitl.

He was outnumbered. His clothes were already soiled from the day's ride and the late night trek through the jungle. It wasn't a matter of the dirt. Jameson had a fear of darkness, a claustrophobia that kept him from entering the tunnel.

"What about the Crystal?" he asked. "I don't want to sever the connection with my soul. What will happen when I reach the chamber?"

"You will follow the path of the light," said Tlacoocelotl. "All you need to do is move the mirrors along the way and it will interrupt the frequency. You will not lose your soul when you enter the Chamber."

"Yes. Trust us," said Papaitl. "If you are worried about changing the frequency, the mirrors can be moved and the light diverted away from tunnel and the Crystal."

"Please," said Ixpetz.

The Cardinal uttered something in Italian, then said a short prayer. His heart thumped in his chest, barely able to contain itself as he thought about what they wanted him to do. He closed his eyes and the past returned to him, a vision of fear that kept him immobile.

He was a young boy playing with his friends. The neighborhood bully and his cronies had cornered them, hounding the younger boys for cheap entertainment. Jameson stood up to them while the younger boys fled. Because he was defiant, they trapped him against a wall. They ripped his clothes as he struggled against them. They dragged him away to an empty lot where an old well was partially covered with a heavy door. With malice they slid the door aside and threw him down the hole.

He began to shout and call for help. They laughed, covering the hole with the door again. Two of the cronies placed a large rock over the door. "This should keep him quiet," they said. Muffled cries came from the hole, drowned by their laughter. Finally they were bored and left the young boy trapped as they wandered off.

"What about the kid?" one of them asked.

"Come on. Let's go find some of his friends. Maybe he'd like some company."

More laughter and mindless agreement followed.

"We'll come back for him later."

But they never planned to.

When you are young, time passes slowly. It cannot be said how long Jameson lay trapped at the bottom of that hole, but for him it was an eternity. He had landed in water and the soft mud beneath it managed to cushion his fall. He did not know if he was bleeding, the cold damp water covered his lower body. He was in pain but it was not from broken bones or deep bruises. He stood in the mud, waist deep. When he struggled he could feel himself slowly sinking deeper in the muck. The walls were somewhat

61

smooth and he saw no way out of this trap. Shouting did not help. His voice echoed off the thick walls of the well, returning to him hollow and empty. With the door covering the hole, freedom lying twenty or thirty feet above, just out of reach, he stood in darkness. It was not long before his eyes grew wet with tears as his limbs uncontrollably began to shiver in the cold, dark water.

His friends had become the hunted. They scattered like dust in the wind, some finding safe paths home, others cowering as they hid and waited.

Young Jameson thought about his predicament. No escape. Hope slowly faded, barely visible in the darkness. His heart sank into the mud like his feet, trapped, held fast in a grasp that tightened with his every movement, his every thought. After the emotions and the tears stopped flowing he turned his thoughts towards heaven and salvation. Everything he had learned about God and angels came to the forefront. God was his only true salvation. He prayed as he had never prayed before, with meaning and not with blind repetition as he did in Sunday church. If there was any light in this darkness, perhaps he could find it in his heart and be saved.

He whispered his petitions, his pleas, his yearnings. Despite his earnest prayers there was no release from his prison. He turned to bargaining, telling God all manner of things he would do if only he survived. He would become an alter boy for Father Kaupon, the parish priest who had tried to recruit him. He would study hard, help his mother and his sisters more, and become a better person. He would learn to fight and defend himself and others. He would devote his life to finding justice and protecting the innocent. He would …

The pleas of the innocent are not unheard. Jameson's life held no bad karma, no lurking evil in his heart. He had simply been a victim. In a world filled with bullies it is inevitable we bump up against them from time to time. Standing up to them builds self confidence and moral fiber, but it can also yield unplanned results.

Like this trauma, hidden deep, waiting to emerge when triggered.

The horrors of the past filled his mind. Jameson stared down that hole in the temple wall. It was as if a storm cloud fell over his heart, blocking the light and threatening all manner of commotion should he enter that abyss. He could see the slime and mud on the floor. It moved and he glimpsed the insects. His mind expanded the vision as he imagined snakes, scorpions, and other deadly things. His heart began to beat stronger. He could feel it in his chest. Blood surged in his temples, pressing into his brain. His breath became rapid and uneven as he gasped uncontrollably. In terror he turned away, moving to an empty patch of wall where he leaned over, coughing and heaving as he tried to regain his composure.

He shut his eyes seeking to focus on nothing. Instead he found himself transported back to that day, back to the bottom of that desolate and hopeless place in his life.

He laid in that well for what seemed like an eternity, his unseen guardian angel as his only company.

One of the boys who ran had witnessed what happened. He hid on a nearby roof watching the older boys throw Jameson into the well. At the sight of it he hid his eyes, fearing he would reveal his position, making him the next target. He heard them shouting but dared not peek over the rooftop. As hard as he wanted to be invisible he knew it was not possible.

The shouting finally died down and he heard them moving away. When he was certain they were gone he peeked over the roof and satisfied his fear that they were not there.

At the bottom of that shaft Jameson had made his last bargain. There was nothing left to offer and a greater darkness began to envelop him. He no longer felt his guardian angel at his side. Instead it was the angel of death.

"So you've come for me, eh?" he said. "Anything is better than this hell I'm in. If this is God's plan for me then I accept it."

The will to live seemed to seep into the water and absorb into the mud. He shivered uncontrollably, his face contorted, the tears beginning to form in his eyes once again. It was becoming difficult for him to stand.

"Please," he said, one last plea on a dying breath. "You heard my promise, God. Let it be life. Let me serve you. It's better for both of us."

He heard a voice from above coming out of the darkness. It was not God, but Biz, his friend who had hidden on the roof. "Carmine? Are you okay?"

"Biz," he shouted. "Help me."

Biz pushed on the rock and managed to roll it aside. He slid the door out of the way. Light streamed down the shaft blinding young Jameson. "I'll go get my dad."

Biz was gone, but Jameson's suffering was not over. He heard voices, and like criminals returning to the scene of a crime, the bullies were back.

"Someone must have set the kid free."

"Too bad."

Heads peered over the sides staring down at him, "No, he's still down there."

"I gotta pee. This place is as good as any."

Laughter. A stream of urine rained down on the small, trapped boy.

"Get out of the way, you punks," came a demanding voice, It was Mr. Bisbee. His friend had returned with reinforcements. There was a sound like meat being tenderized, then yelps and cries from the bullies, then a new voice. "Yeah, go tell your Dad I hit you. You're lucky I don't throw you down this shaft."

He saw his Father look down the hole and the rescue was on.

A few days went by before Carmine Jameson was able to review what happened. As far as his pleas and prayers to God were concerned, he decided a bargain is a bargain, even when made under duress. Out of that darkness came a decision to follow the path of Light, to devote his life to God and to the spiritual evolution of humanity. Yet, the terror remained with him.

Trauma, when it is not processed and released, sometimes buries itself. It likes to lodge itself in the back side of the chakras, sometimes manifesting as unexplained emotions from the heart. It hides in the mind creating fear and doubt. It strikes in the gut where it immobilizes and blocks the ability to move forward.

All which affected him now.

"I can't do it," he said, turning to leave.

"Yes, you can," said Tlacoocelotl. "I see your memories and how they eclipse your courage. It has rooted you in the past and frozen your body. You must move forward, beyond the trauma. Think! Think about what happened next, how your life changed for the better."

"Yes," whispered the Cardinal. His eyes remained closed, his memory sharp and clear. "Yes."

Ixpetz and Papaitl looked towards the sacred cat.

"Let me help you," said Tlacoocelotl. "I am a spirit guide. I can heal you. All you have to do is ask. Give me permission."

Jameson looked down the hole, then at Tlacoocelotl. Was he going mad? Seeing and talking to invisible beings! What was happening to him? Was he becoming psychic or going crazy?

With a heavy breath he said, "Okay. Heal me. Take this affliction and this doubt from me."

Tlacoocelotl gave him no quarter. The ocelot leaped toward him, claws extended, teeth bared. Jameson was terrified as he fell backwards. The ghost-like image of Tlacoocelotl entered his body and a surge of strength and courage filled his being. He wanted to roar like a jungle cat. In his heart there was no room for fear, in his gut no more barriers. He took several deep breaths. With newfound determination he pulled himself up and entered the small dark corridor that led to the center of the temple.

Chapter 14

A Surprise Visitor

The airport was crowded. The Eighth Day Village of the Sun was hosting a conference and, in addition to the usual stream of tourists, a steady flow of smart dressed businessmen and women passed through the main portal.

"Where are all these people coming from?" asked Christine.

"The kiosk says there are a number of private flights that brought all these folks here. Expect crowded conditions. That explains all the extra trams lined up outside," said Manny. He looked out at the planes on the tarmac. There were two jumbo jets still unloading passengers. Beyond that there was a field of parked airplanes. "Check it out," he said, pointing. "All those private jets and planes. Lots of wealthy people must be here too." He laughed. "The first thing Randall built when he established the Eighth Day Village of the Sun was an air conditioned conference center."

"I guess it turned out pretty successful," said Christine. "What is this conference about?"

"It's a technology thing," said Manny. "A new development in personal hardware. It's all hush hush for now. I was briefed on the Think Tank but I can't really talk about it."

"Who are we looking for again?" asked Christine.

"Professor Barnheart," he said. "He should be easy to spot. He'll have two young children with him that are barely teenagers, the Gorgofsky twins." He showed her a photo of them on his communicator.

"Where do you know this professor?"

"He was one of my college profs. He primarily taught

chemistry but also physics. We kind of had an affinity for each other and we became friends."

"What's he doing here?"

"He lives in the Village now," said Manny. "We both lecture at the Village Research Center. He teaches psychic chemistry, a field he actively researches."

"What's that? What exactly is psychic chemistry?"

"It's using the power of your mind to drive chemical reactions," explained Manny. "He can psychically manipulate and transform molecules with his mental acuity."

"No way," she said.

"Oh yes. It's true. Why wouldn't it be? Energy drives all chemical reactions. Psychic energy is just as potent as heat or light. Barnheart is bringing back the ancient art of alchemy and updating it for modern times."

"Interesting," said Christine. She continued to scan the crowd with Manny. "These twins, you know them?"

"Uh huh," he said.

"What's so important about them?"

"They built the temple in New Maya," said Manny, his eyes focused on the streaming masses of people.

"Cool," she said. "Like a playhouse or something?"

"No. It's a life sized temple. It was in ruins and they rebuilt it. I got to see them work on it. They're pretty talented for young kids." He smiled. "Look! There they are!"

Barnheart lit up like a Christmas tree upon seeing Manny. He rushed forward moving through the crowd with the twins in tow. "Manfred," he said, wrapping his friend in a bear hug of an embrace.

"Please don't call me that. It's Manny."

"Yes, yes," said Barnheart.

"Christine, this is my old friend and colleague, Dr. Maximilian Barnheart."

"You can call me Max," said Barnheart. "Especially if Manfred lets you call him Manny."

"Everyone does," said Manny. "Everyone but him."

The twins rushed forward, a young boy and a girl doing the same. Manny enjoyed the hugs, accepting their love as a gift to be cherished and enjoyed.

"I hear you're taking us to New Maya City of Worlds," said Yorgi.

"In a crystal ship again," added Petra.

"Yes I am," said Manny. "Christine, may I introduce Yorgi and Petra, the Gorgofsky twins."

"I hope we don't crash like last time," said Yorgi.

"Crash?" said Christine.

"I've heard so much about you," said Barnheart, diverting the subject. "Nice to meet you." He gave her equal treatment, his welcoming hug just as loving and all embracing. He released her, spying an impeccably dressed dark haired woman poised with confidence and standing patiently behind Manny. "Ah, and I see Donna is with you, too."

Manny turned around, surprised and shocked. He and Christine had been so focused on the crowd that they never noticed her behind them. "I've been standing here for the last five minutes listening to you two jabber, waiting for my chance to break in."

"I'm sorry," said Christine. "Donna, is it?" She extended her hand in greeting.

The blood drained from Manny's head. His stomach churned like a front loading washing machine.

Donna looked at Christine's hand like it was a wet dishrag.

"Well?" said Donna staring at Manny.

"Christine, may I introduce Donna Pallatzio, formerly Donna Dubois, my ex-wife."

"Oh," said Christine.

Chapter 15

The Stygian Abyss

Carmine Jameson crawled down the dark tunnel. Light streamed around his form partially illuminating the way ahead. It did not encourage him. It cast moving shadows across the walls and ceiling, creepy patterns of competing light and dark. There was moss. Bugs and ants bit him. Mud made him slide at times as the shaft sloped downward. The temple had been recently constructed but it seemed that it didn't take long for the jungle to move in.

Ahead there was an obstruction. He came to a mirror and a lens. He pushed on it and it seemed to ride along on some kind of track. The tunnel opened up to the right revealing a larger space beside him. It was tall enough to stand and his joints ached. He moved to the side and slid off. "I'm still tired from the hike we had to make to get here," he said, standing as he complained to no one in particular.

There was a short walk past the lens where there was another mirror. There were two tunnels offering him a choice. "Which way now?"

"Follow the path of the Light," he heard in his head. "It will lead to the Ascension Chamber."

He studied the path ahead and moved the mirror aside. This tunnel was much cleaner and less terrifying, but it became dark and foreboding after he moved the mirror. From here on, there would be no light.

Once again he hoisted himself up and into that hole, following a conviction that he could somehow make it to his friend and help. He had no idea what he would do. Maybe pray. He was a priest after all. He thought about his own plight, the trauma of his youth that had put him on the path to becoming a priest. He summoned the courage of a mountain lion, or in this case a jungle ocelot, and began the slow crawl down yet another tunnel.

The blackness began to cover his heart. His breath became sharp and staccato. He shut his eyes and stopped moving for a moment. Platitudes began to fill his mind. *There is nothing in the darkness that wasn't there before in the light.*

What about the Crystal? Is it really safe? I don't want to enter the chamber and find myself separated from my immortal soul.

"My angels," he called aloud. "I know you're here. Be with me now."

He moved his hand forward, first one then another, his knees following the rhythm. God how they hurt! He had forgotten all about his rear end aching from the horse ride. His calf muscles strained from the hike. There was a new pain growing in his knees from crawling on the stone. Without the mud his pants gave him no cushion against the rough surface of rock.

Thinking about the pain in his knees became a distraction. He no longer held on to fear and instead inched forward, thinking to himself as he moved.

Why this psychic stuff? I'm not some carnival fortune teller. I'm a priest! A Catholic Cardinal. What would the Vatican say about me? Have I gone renegade? Too much exposure to this Village and these new ideas!

His thoughts ran in circles. Doubt filled the darkness ahead of him. The tunnel seemed endless, his progress minuscule. There was an obstruction ahead. He stopped and felt around it, perhaps a mirror or a lens, but something in the way. *How do I get past this?* He pushed on it but it was attached somewhere and strongly anchored to the wall.

The tunnel angled to his right. The mirror was one that was used to reflect light down a new path. He twisted his body, wedging himself beside it, thankful he was a skinny priest and not a fat friar. The mirror was rigid, his body flexible. Despite his contortions, halfway through the restriction he got stuck.

Panic spread through him like a gas lit flame. His breath grew quick and shallow.

Stop it, Carmine, he heard a voice say. *Calm down. You're letting fear get the best of you.*

"Who said that?" he asked. "Is there someone behind me?"

His own voice echoed off the thick walls of the tunnel. There was no one. No answer.

No matter. It was good advice. "Calm down," he said to himself. His breath grew slower and he noticed how slim he felt when his breath was shallow and his lungs empty. He could almost feel enough room to squirm through the restriction.

And thinking made it so, just as it always does. Where there is a will, there is a way.

Jameson laughed as he once again moved down the tunnel. "Ha! If I don't make it as a side show psychic I could still become a contortionist."

His voice came back hollow, an empty echo returned by the stone.

In his head he heard. *Keep moving. You are urgently needed.*

"Who said that?" he asked. Again, no reply. He started moving, his back joining in with the chorus of body aches he now felt. "This psychic thing is crazy," he said. "Now I'm hearing voices and seeing ghosts."

A strange complaint from someone who has been seeing and talking to angels his whole life.

"Yes, but the angels don't talk back like you do. Whoever you are."

Oh, but they do talk to you. Your spirit is always listening. You unconsciously hear them. Now, because you have been expanding and focusing your awareness, you can actually hear them.

"And these ghosts? Why do I see them?"

Because they want you to. Accept your gifts, Carmine. Being psychic is not a circus game, it is the beginning of perception.

His confidence returned. There were no more restrictions in the tunnel. He came to a point where he reached forward into empty space. There were candles illuminating the Chamber. He saw the prone body of Kamala Singh lying on the floor.

Carmine Jameson slipped out of the abyss and into the dim light of the Ascension Chamber.

Chapter 16

Exes and Ohs

"Donna Pallatzio?" said Christine. "The famous model?"

"That's her," said Manny nervously.

"And you were married to *her*?"

The two women stared at each other for a moment before Barnheart broke the tension. "So, we are off on another adventure?"

"It would seem so," said Manny.

"Yay!" shouted the twins.

"I spoke with Randall. He said he needs us in New Maya," said Barnheart.

"Then we better get going," said Manny. "We have a ship reserved. Come on." He turned towards Donna. "Well, it was good to see you..."

She interrupted him. "And you're going to keep seeing me. I came here because we have business to discuss."

"Business?"

"Yes!" she insisted.

"It will have to wait. I don't have time for it, Donna. Didn't you hear? We're on an important mission."

"Oh, it's not so important," said Barnheart. He turned towards Donna. "These are the Gorgofsky twins, Petra and Yorgi. I'm just taking them to New Maya City of Worlds. They built a temple there and somebody accidentally got locked up in it. Manny is flying us there in a crystal ship."

"Oooh," said Donna. "Sounds like fun. I'm in."

74

"What?" said Manny.

Before he could say anything else Barnheart broke in. "Wonderful. It will give us time to catch up."

Manny glared at Barnheart. The old man just smiled back at him. Donna sported her model perfect fake smile. My God! How do you get teeth that white? Christine shifted nervously from foot to foot as the Gorgofsky twins gathered around Manny.

"I'm looking forward to another ride in your crystal ship," said Yorgi.

"Me, too," added Petra.

His hesitation was brief until Manny said, "Okay. I have a shuttle ready to take us to the crystal skyport. Let's load up."

Barnheart raised his arm holding his bag. "I travel light," he said.

"We have all our stuff too," said the twins pointing to their backpacks.

Donna motioned to a thin man standing nonchalantly nearby. He held an electronic device that he stared at for a moment. He looked up and nodded. Manny had nothing to say, just turned and headed towards a counter marked overhead with the words TRANSPORT. There was a long line, suits and tourists standing impatiently. Manny walked past the counter waving his communicator. "Good morning, Teresa, I have a reservation. Party of 6. Four adults, two children..."

"...don't forget my photographer, darling," said Donna. She flashed those whiter than whites again, voicing his name and gesturing as an introduction. "Peter B. Coterie."

The lady behind the counter winked and smiled. "Where to this time, Manny?"

"Short hop over to the crystal ships then on to New Maya."

"When are you going to take me for a ride," she said, her voice taking on a sultry drawl, her eyes suddenly soft and inviting.

He got lost in it for a moment, staring through her deep brown irises. "Soon," he said. "Thanks, Teresa. You're a saint." He broke away from her gaze, the moment witnessed by everyone in eyesight. She smiled back and tapped a button on the underside of the counter opening a door behind her.

"Am I going to get that kind of service?" asked a tall man in a brown suit, the next in line.

"Of course," said Teresa. She extended a finger, wiggling it for him to come to her. Like Manny, he melted into her eyes, becoming a pool of liquid putty. "Now, what's you're name handsome and what can I do for you?"

The next man in line turned to the one behind him. "This is going to be worth the wait."

"You said it," came the response.

The Dubois Party went through the door and down a long corridor, Peter B. Coterie pushing a heavy cart of baggage behind them.

"Where do you know her?" asked Christine, her head nodding back towards Teresa. "Sounds like she works more than the transport counter."

"She comes to the Bistro every now and then," he answered. "Everyone in the Village does. Eventually."

"Manny was always popular," interjected Donna.

The photographer grunted, pushing the cart.

"Are you planning on moving here?" asked Manny. "What have you got in there?"

"Barely enough for the week. Don't worry. I'll be out of your hair before you know it. Maybe sooner, after you hear my business."

"Why don't you just tell me what it is," said Manny. "Then you won't even need to be here."

She chuckled, touching his cheek gently. "What I have to offer will be said in private."

"There's nothing you can offer me, Donna," said Manny, "Our relationship served its purpose."

"Don't be too sure," she said.

Christine gave him a quick glance. They reached the end of the corridor and he held the door open for her. There was a waiting shuttle and they loaded up quickly.

The crystal ship had been prepped. The dirigible like balloon was fully inflated. It added some ballast to the ship, but it was the anti gravity technology licensed from the Galactics that actually kept the ship afloat. They boarded the clear crystal gondola. Manny and Yorgi helped Peter load and stow the luggage in the baggage compartment.

"You must have a lot of camera equipment," said Yorgi.

"Oh, no," said Peter. He pointed to a small case. "This is all I have. The rest of this belongs to Ms. Pallatzio."

Inside the ship conversation was terse.

"So, you are a model?" asked Petra.

"Yes, little one," said Donna, patting her head as if she were a pet collie. "I get to wear lots of pretty clothes and travel all over the world."

"Donna Pallatzio," said Christine. "Weren't you the one Richard Sooka said was too fat to model?"

"No. You have me confused with Zanzibar O'Connel," she said, narrowing her eyes. "I was actually married to Richard Sooka."

Christine gasped. "The famous designer? Wasn't he murdered? Something to do with the show he was a judge on, *Designer Derby*, wasn't it?"

"That was some time ago," said Donna. "Let's forget the past. There is so much more to talk about now. Like, how long have you and Manny been an item?"

Christine looked down and through the transparent floor of the ship. "I wouldn't say we're an item." She looked up at Donna.

"A relationship is not an item, at least not to me."

"I see."

Barnheart joined in. "I followed some of your career after you graduated, Donna."

"You can't help it," she replied. "I'm big on social media."

"Yes," said Barnheart. "I always wondered why you chose modeling over physics. You were an excellent student."

"I'm sorry I disappointed you, Professor," she said. "I just found that modeling was more lucrative than teaching or doing research. Also I don't have to write lengthy papers that few people will read. I don't engage in open debate about what I am studying. It's so much easier to put on a dress and have people take pictures of me." She got up and did a quick spin and a runway pose. She was wearing the latest in high fashion, an illuminated dress that clung to her frame like cellophane to yesterday's vegetables. Christine couldn't help but notice her muscles, chiseled to perfection, the result of years of eastern yoga and western exercise.

"Wow," said Petra.

"After you got your masters in Quantum Mechanics I thought for sure you would continue on to your doctorate like Manfred did."

"Physics was always Manny's field, not mine," said Donna. "I lost interest in physics when he lost interest in me. He chose subatomic particles over the genuine article. Me!" She huffed and sat down.

"You majored in physics in college?" asked Christine.

"Please," said Donna. "Let's forget the past! Can't you people move on and live in the present?"

Manny, Peter and Yorgi broke the tension as they entered the cabin. "Well, are we all settled in?" asked Manny.

There were stares and some smiles. Manny looked at Donna flashing her smile. It was hard to stop the floodgate of memories that poured from the depths of his mind. *Things best forgotten*, he thought. He looked at Christine. She was hard to read. He couldn't fathom what she was thinking. She looked uncomfortable, to say the least. "All right then," he said. "Let me start the preflight check and we'll be on our way."

It wasn't long before they were airborne. The tension seemed to fade as the crystal ship cleared the hanger and slowly turned towards New Maya City of Words. Visitors at the airport gawked at the sight of it.

"I hear they grow the crystal cabins and attach them to the balloon," said one tourist.

"I'd love to get a ride on one," said another.

"I tried," said a third. "I offered a ridiculous sum of money and they refused."

"Didn't you know? Money doesn't mean that much in the Eighth Day Village of the Sun."

"How savage," said a well dressed man.

As the ship flew over the jungle, conversation was replaced with sightseeing. With a flip of a switch the walls turned completely transparent and passengers were able to view the landscape below. There were distant mountains, an occasional lake, and meadows filled with wildlife.

Soon, New Maya City of Worlds came into view. It was a jungle city carved out of the wilderness. People could be seen moving across the catwalks and bridges that joined the tall trees and formed the main thoroughfares of New Maya. Long ago as more homes and shops were located high in the trees, engineers built walkways and bridges to join these structures. Parts of the system were living things, constructed in the same manner as the bridges in the East Khasi Hills of India. New Maya technology allowed plants to grow quickly, avoiding centuries of tedious pruning and guidance. Tourists found it enchanting. Locals found it necessary.

The Temple of the Ascension Crystal dominated the landscape, the tall structure rising above everything. There was an open field next to the temple and Manny guided the crystal ship towards a gentle landing on the grassy plain. Randall was talking with two guards at the temple entrance. When he saw the crystal highliner landing, he stopped and hurried towards the ship. Barnheart and the twins were just debarking when he arrived.

"We are here," said Barnheart. "Now, what is the big emergency Mr. Randall?"

"It's those two guards," said Randall. "They won't let us into the temple."

"Isn't that their job?" asked Petra.

"To keep the tourists out," said Randall. "Not us. Besides, I have a permit to enter." He waved the writ in front of them. "Signed by the Council of Elders."

Donna stepped out of the ship. Randall could not stop staring at her. As a holy man he shouldn't be distracted, but she was beautiful and so elegantly dressed. "This will do nicely," she said turning to her photographer. "Peter, deploy the personal drones. I'm ready to start broadcasting."

"Who are you?" asked Randall.

She started to extend a hand but instead went for a kiss on the cheek. "Donna Pallatzio, darling."

"And what are you doing here?"

Manny finished powering down the ship and joined them. "I don't believe you've had the pleasure. Randall, may I introduce my ex-wife."

"Pleased," she said, flippant and uninterested. "Peter, get those drones out. This is perfect. We'll shoot with the temple in the background. Hurry, the morning light is fading."

Randall shook his head and gave Manny a discerning look. "We have a crisis on our hands," he said.

"I expected no less," said Manny, thinking, *Isn't it always a crisis?*

Christine was the last to leave the ship. She scanned the area. "What a beautiful place!" She locked her arm in Manny's. "Thank you for bringing me here." She gave him a peck on the cheek.

"I was on vacation break when you called, Randall," said Manny. "You said to get here quickly. I had to bring Christine to make it happen. Besides, she can help with..." he looked around. "...Whatever it is."

"And your ex-wife?" asked Randall. "Why is she here, of all people?"

Barnheart came to his defense. "I invited her along. She had urgent business with Manfred and I didn't want to delay things. It seemed okay at the time."

Randall shook his head. He squatted down to eye level with the twins. "So good of you to come," he said.

"We were finished at Uxmal," said Yorgi.

"Their temple is not as magical as ours," said Petra. She smiled looking past the guards at the magnificent structure they had built.

"You said something about a person locked inside the temple," said Barnheart.

"Yes," said Randall. "In the Ascension Chamber. It's Kamala Singh. Let's get moving. I'll explain along the way."

There wasn't much to gather up. "I'm going to leave my stuff in the ship," said Barnheart. "I'll keep this water though." He went through his luggage and stuffed his pockets with a few items. A compass, knife, a notebook, a pencil, and a few other essentials. As they all walked away, Donna remained behind. Manny glanced back, half expecting to be turned into a pillar of salt, but he was relieved to be away from her.

Randall tried arguing with the temple guards one more time. They refused to stand away from the door and let them enter.

"Isn't there a high priest, a clergyman we can talk to?

Look!" He held the paper out. "I have a writ granting me entry by the Council."

"I'm sorry sir my orders come from the High Priestess herself."

"Yes, She is the one I'm here to see."

The answer came with abrupt finality. "She is busy now. She asked not to be disturbed. Come back later."

Randall gave up and joined the group, moving them out of ear shot of the guards. "You see why I asked you to come here, children. Can you help me get into the temple?"

"There is another way," said Yorgi.

"At the top of the pyramid," said Petra.

"I'm depending on you," he said to the twins. "I need your knowledge of the temple."

Petra smiled. "Okay."

"We built it after all," said Yorgi.

The comment shook Christine. She had imagined a kid's playhouse, not this massive stone structure. "How did you ever build this?" she asked.

"It's a long story," said Barnheart.

"Yes," urged Randall. "Let's get moving."

"We have to climb up there?" asked Christine.

"You can stay here or go back to the ship," said Manny.

She locked her arm is his. "No way. I'm on this tour too."

Chapter 17

A Higher Council

The inter dimensional tsunami wave started small and simple at the Ascension Crystal, yet it grew and traveled far, leaving damage in its wake. At one point there was a crack in the heavens and a rumble of thunder. It shook like an earthquake, tossed like an angry sea, and fell like a mudslide that covered and silenced the Elysian Fields. Light faded and darkness crept into every empty space available.

And yet there was no sound, no movement in the Chamber of the Ascension Crystal. No fierce wind and no quaking beneath the prone form of Kamala Singh. It was the higher dimensions that trembled in darkness. The Crystal, to fulfill the process of severing the soul of Kamala Singh, had cleaved into the higher realms and shattered them into chaos. It had created a place where God could not see, a place of darkness so void that it spilled into multiple dimensions and places. There was imbalance in the universe and no place to hide from it.

And so the call went out to the higher dimensional beings. Beyond the fifth dimension, beyond the Ascended Masters, beyond even the level of the souls striving and moving between the endless Sea of Love and the physical plane of incidence.

From within that Divine Sea of Love shapes began to emerge, liquid beings encased in Light as they formed into a group consciousness. A single purpose surfaced as they moved away and left the Sea behind.

We must now call the Council of Souls to order. Let us freeze galactic time beneath the Firmament of duality until we decide what to do about this breach. With our Divine purpose and will, we now create a pocket universe on the Earth to continue the drama that shaped this cataclysm. Let us observe, contemplate and comprehend the many possibilities and witness the outcome. Then we can restore peace to the atomic universe and balance to the etheric realms that rest upon it. Let the Council convene.

Chapter 18

The Golem

Kamala Singh was unconscious. Cardinal Jameson went right to her side. He was glad that he was trained in first aid. He checked her heartbeat and respiration and found neither. His first thought was to start CPR.

"She's dead!" he cried out loud. "But for how long?" He felt her neck and it was warm. "Not long I think." He bent down, preparing to deliver two lifesaving breaths. When their lips met she revived instantly.

She reached behind his head and held it fast, delivering a passionate kiss. Jameson jerked back, surprised by the quick move.

"Eh? What are you doing? I thought you were dead."

She didn't answer and instead stared back at him. He felt uneasy. There was something in her eyes. He had remembered them full of life, lit with intent and purpose. That light seemed to be gone.

There was an odd smell in the chamber. He couldn't fathom it at first. Upon inspection he saw she had urinated on herself. "Should we clean that up?" he asked.

She continued to stare.

"Can I help you, Kamala? Are you okay? What do you need?"

Her limbs tensed, her muscles tightened.

Jameson felt a reassuring hand on his shoulder. The ghosts of the past were with him. In his heart there was the sudden surge of courage, a jungle cat facing a challenge.

"Singh! What happened?" he demanded.

She murmured like a child, like a stroke victim, bubbles of spittle forming on her lips.

He thought she was whispering something. He moved nearer, putting his ear close to her mouth. There was nothing clear and recognizable. With a sudden lunge, she jerked up and bit his ear. He drew back, his hand covering the small trickle of blood. He stood up, looking down at her. "What's wrong with you!" he shouted. "What would make you do something like that? I just crawled through hell to help you. And this is how you act?"

His anger flared and then abated. He had the heart of a priest after all. He turned slightly, keeping an eye on her while he composed himself. *She is not herself*, he thought. *This is some kind of strange condition or disease.* He pulled his hand away from his ear, wiping the blood on his shirt. *She is like an animal. Has she lost her soul already? Am I too late?*

She looked up at the Cardinal, sultry and inviting. "Did you know what a handsome man you are?"

"Oh, so you can speak now," he said.

"When I want to."

"What do you mean by that?"

She leaned in close. "Just..."

Jameson shuddered, then pointed to his collar. "I'm a priest for God's sake."

"Priests are just men in special clothes," she said. "Or are you the kind that likes little boys?"

"Neither," he scorned. "I am dedicated to my vows! I haven't broken them in thirty years."

She went in for the kiss again. She reached out to stroke his leg. He avoided both.

"Can someone explain to me what's going on?" he asked.

He heard a voice in his head. *Protect yourself, Carmine.*

Jameson said a brief prayer, calling upon his guardian

angel and all the archangels that could hear him. "What's going on here?" he said. "You're not at all acting like Singh."

Tlacoocelotl emerged from his heart and appeared beside him. Kamala looked at the ocelot and hissed. "What is this magic?" she said. Her eyes became dark and she went to lunge at the jungle cat.

The ocelot was quick. It jumped between Kamala and Jameson, roaring and threatening her with his powerful claws. Kamala made a move and before he knew it Jameson was watching a cat fight, one like nobody had ever seen. All manner of thoughts went through his head. *Is this real? How can a higher dimensional cat interact with the real world? Is Kamala real or am I actually going crazy?*

There was a blur and both of them disappeared. When he looked down he saw the body of Kamala Singh laying quietly on the floor. He bent down beside her again. The body was cold. "What is this strangeness?" he asked.

He walked over to the Crystal, shouting at it. "What about you? What have you done this time?" He looked back at Kamala. "Is there a way to undo this?" He grasped the handle that rotated the Crystal. He started to push on it but suddenly reconsidered. "I know what you're capable of," he said to it. "I don't want you taking my soul away or any other strange magic." His hand tightened on the handle for a moment. "But where would I move you?" He looked down at Kamala. "She would know. She understands how to use you. I am like a child holding a hand grenade." He let go of the handle. "I remember what you did to me in the Point of Departure. Not just me, the entire population of New Maya City of Worlds. We don't want a repeat of that." He spotted a lump of cloth on the floor. It was a dark velvet covering used to hide the Crystal from light. "This should stop you from any more mischief." He spread it out and worked it over the top of the Crystal, then went back to the side of Kamala Singh.

There was a voice behind him, or was it in his head? Tlacoocelotl attempted to explain it to him. *She has severed the connection to her soul. Her connection to God was through that soul. For the moment the connection is still active but it is dissolving. That was not Kamala Singh. It was a negative entity using her form for its own gratification. Fortunately I was able to fight it off, but if it comes back I may need your help.*

"For what? What can I do? Some kind of exorcism?" asked the Cardinal. "I'm afraid I'm not that kind of priest."

Listen, Father. Priest. Whatever you are. There is not much time to ask. What do you do when a soul becomes lost and disconnected from God?

The answer was obvious to Jameson. "Why, I pray for its salvation."

And aren't you in the business of saving souls? asked Tlacoocelotl. *That is what you modern day priests do, correct?*

"Yes, it is."

Well, then I would say you're the perfect person for the job. It's why you're here. Get busy. Save a soul, for God's sake.

Chapter 19

One Step at a Time

Barnheart and the Gorgofsky twins stood before the temple stairs.

"We have to go up there," said Yorgi, pointing.

"Oh, goody," said Petra. "It's nice and cool up there."

"Can't you just move a stone down here or something?" asked Barnheart. "Make a hole so we can get into the temple another way. Why do we need to climb all the way up to the top?"

"The stones are happy where they are," said Petra. "They rest and rely upon one another."

"If we moved a stone the temple may become unstable," said Yorgi.

"Yes, yes," said Barnheart. "I understand physics. Surely not every stone is a keystone."

"There's an easy way in up there," said Petra. "All we have to do is climb these stairs."

Barnheart sighed. "Easy for you to say."

"It's okay Professor," said Yorgi. "Just take your time. We'll stay with you."

"Yes, yes," said Barnheart. "Thank you." They were narrow steps of stone, not quite the size and width of modern stairs. He carefully navigated a few steps. "Why didn't you make the steps normal sized when you built this temple?"

Petra laughed. "They are normal. They are the same size as the temples at Uxmal and Cancun. You know that."

"We just followed the blueprint given to us in the Point of

Departure," said Yorgi.

"I'm sorry, children. It's a beautiful temple. I'm just complaining like an old man."

The twins laughed. "Come on, then," said Petra, taking his hand. "We'll climb with you, slow and easy."

"If we leave now, maybe the others will catch up to us," said Yorgi. "And there's a nice place to rest at the top."

Barnheart grunted, lifting his foot almost knee high and placing it on the thin stone in front of him. "How many steps?" he asked, adding, "Never mind. I don't want to know." He looked down at his feet, entering into a rhythm of step, grunt, step, grunt, and so on.

Manny was passing idle talk with Christine when Randall joined them, stressing the urgency of the situation. "Cardinal Jameson is already up there," he said. "He may already be inside the temple. I asked him to see if he could gain access and check on Singh."

"You mentioned that Singh was in danger," said Christine. "Something about her severing the connection to her soul. Is that even possible?"

"With the Ascension Crystal anything is possible. Reliable sources have told me what Singh is up to."

"Reliable sources?" questioned Manny.

Randall also wondered why he had used the term *reliable sources* when referencing Tlacoocelotl, Ixpetz and Papaitl. Nonetheless, he said, "Maybe I should have said a *higher authority*. Anyway, I trust my sources. All the more reason to hurry. Let's get going."

Christine tried to suppress a laugh as she dug her face into Manny's chest.

"What? What is it?" asked Manny.

There was a hum as a tiny drone circled him. It was annoying, like a housefly only bigger, more like the size of a small bird. He swatted at it.

"Hey, watch it. Those are my personal drones. They're very expensive."

It was Donna, his ex-wife. He saw what Christine was laughing at. She was dressed in a harem costume or some kind of belly dancing garb. It was comical. He turned away to hide his face from her as he also suppressed a laugh.

"Did I hear something about rescuing someone's soul?" she said. "Is it true?"

Randall shook his head and turned, beginning to climb the steps.

"What's with that outfit?" asked Manny.

"Well, we are exploring a temple," she said.

"And your Laura Croft clothes were at the cleaners?" asked Manny.

Donna sneered at him, directing her conversation to a second drone that circled close to her. "That's my ex-husband, Manny Dubois. My first ex-husband. I'm here with this team of people getting ready to climb these stairs and enter the Sacred Temple of the Ascension Crystal." She looked towards Manny. "Isn't that right, Honey?"

"Don't call me that," said Manny. "I'm not your honey. Not anymore."

"Ah, still bitter," said Donna. She turned towards the drone. "Our breakup was an absolute minefield of destruction. He had trouble dealing with losing me. Who wouldn't?"

Manny shook his head. He swatted at the nearest drone. "What are these things?"

"My personal recorders," she said. "They are attached to Artificial Intelligence which edits and posts these comments to my twenty four hour sites."

"You broadcast all night?"

"You'd be amazed at the number of people who like to watch me sleep, darling," she said.

"They probably imagine they are sleeping with you, my dear," said Peter, faithful photographer and pack animal. He was loaded down as usual. He scowled at Manny. "Stop swatting at the drones. I only brought a few replacements."

"So glad you're here, Peter Darling," said Donna. She turned to Manny. "Well! Didn't I hear someone say it was urgent? There's a soul or something at stake." She swept her hands as if she were scattering insects on a hot summer day. "Let's get moving people."

Manny got ready to let loose a slur of comments. A drone momentarily blocked his view of her as it hovered nearby focusing on him. He caught sight of Christine. She gave him a slight nod and Manny realized he was now a public spectacle. He went back to smiling. He took her hand gently in his and turned, walking up the steps with her.

They could hear Donna talking as she followed behind them, her kitten heels clacking on the stone with every step. "For those of you new to my channel, Manny and I met in graduate school. Yes, I was a college nerd at one time, but after my disappointing marriage to Manny Dubois I began to study men instead of natural science." She winked at the cameras. "A more interesting subject, I might add. Men are infinitely simpler than particle physics. Take my ex here for example. See how his new girlfriend leads him around by the hand, holding it like she would a child's. The question I would ask is who is holding who?"

Manny turned around. "Would you just stop it!" he demanded.

"See?" said Donna. "What we have here is the male reaction to being called out. Notice how, in confronting me, he has let go of mommy's hand, abandoning her to stroke his male pride and ego."

Christine reached for his hand but he didn't take it. Instead he quickened his pace as he continued up the steps. Christine did a double step and caught up to him.

"Note the wounded bear response," said Donna. "You see the same behavior in elementary school boys who have no idea how to handle criticism, let alone the emotions that come with this kind of reaction."

Drones circled him, trying to catch a glimpse of his face. He swatted at them like flies, their buzzing only increasing his irritation.

"Hey, stop that," yelled Peter.

Donna continued talking. "We were engaged in graduate school and married soon after we both got our Masters degrees. But you loyal fans already know that story. Everything changes after you're married. The romance and dating phase of the relationship is over and its time to get down to business. At least that's what some people think." She shot a discerning glance towards her ex, a gesture caught by the drones and transmitted to millions of eager fans.

Manny and Christine continued up the stairs trying to ignore her by focusing on the steep climb.

"Manny Dubois had different ideas of what marriage would be like," said Donna. "And that was only the beginning of our differences. Yes, I majored in physics, even did some graduate work in Europe. He expected me to be some kind of research wife like Marie Curie where we would work together and discover the Rosetta Stone of modern science." She stopped climbing for a moment and turned towards one of the drones. "Marie died of radiation poisoning, you know. Ah, the rewards of front line science and the true cost of discovery." She started climbing again, slow and graceful, her elaborate costume flowing about her as if it had a life of its own. "After graduate school, Manfred..." she let out a chuckle, "...as he liked to call himself in those days, attended some high brow German university where he had a fellowship. I can't remember the name of the place, but it was incredibly stuffy and boring."

Manny stopped climbing, turned around and shouted back at her. "It was he Julius Maximilians University in Würzburg for God's sake. I was working on my doctorate in Quantum Engineering. Have you forgotten everything?"

Donna smiled. "Oh, so you have been listening to me. Do you have any more comments about our marriage? Or about anything? For my fans, of course. I'm sure they'd love to hear what you have to say."

Christine gave him a look as she brushed past him. Manny didn't know what to say. He stood as motionless as a mouse being stalked by a cat. He suddenly didn't know which way to turn.

Donna walked past him next, her smile wry and confident. "Confused, little man? The top is this way." Peter, her faithful photographer and pack animal, followed close behind, leaving Manny in last place. She continued to spin words as she weaved her story. "Now, where was I? Oh, yes. Manfred spent all his time at the Gluteus Maximus University in Würzburg trying to impress his colleagues and professors. It was our honeymoon and it fizzled like a bad experiment. I thought it was me. Imagine that!" She chuckled for effect.

"He wanted me to come down to his lab and work with him, conduct and manage all these little projects he was working on, be his little secretary. He never seemed to pick up on the fact that I wasn't interested in science anymore. I wanted to be a wife and mother, one of the top reasons many people get married. I tried science. I worked for a while but I was bored and ready to move on. I began to study fashion. He thought I was reading research papers but I was looking at magazines. I improved my wardrobe, increased my makeup skills, even went all culinary. Do you think he would pay attention to me? He'd come home talking all excited about quantum pairing and the Schrödinger equation. I wanted to quit the marriage before it even got started."

"You did!" shouted Manny. The drones were around him again, waiting to record more of his comments. He bit his lip and focused on his climbing instead.

Donna continued her litany. "You see his reaction, all tense and defensive. I mean, a little yin, a little yang, it's good for the relationship. but this was pathetic. Anyway, it was less than four hours by train to Paris, the center of the world for fashion, and I wound up going there to get away from the miserable circumstances I had gotten into. He didn't even notice I was gone for two weeks,"

"It was two days," shouted Manny.

"Glad you're still paying attention to me, darling," said Donna.

"Why don't you just shut up," said Manny. "I don't know how you can talk and climb at the same time. Don't you ever get tired or winded?"

"You obviously haven't seen any of my exercise videos or workout routines, otherwise you'd do less huffing and puffing." She turned towards the nearest drone. "For those of you that *are* interested in fitness and well-being, my workout videos are available on my channel twenty four hours a day. There are a healthy assortment of free ones so you can work out with me at no cost. Come on, darlings. In a few short weeks you can be looking like this."

She stopped climbing, striking a model pose, then changing to a few others. The drones did their work and Peter held Manny back so he wouldn't foul things up and ruin the shot. They exchanged angry glances.

Manny pushed past him. Donna blocked him by moving fluidly into another model pose. With her feet planted firmly, hands on her hips and a defiant smile, it was quite effective. As Manny tried to move around her, she countered, looking like a graceful belly dancer as she shifted and shimmied from side to side.

Manny stopped struggling and said, "I don't know why I agreed to bring you along with us. You're being a total nuisance."

"Oh, no, darling. It's you who's being the nuisance."

"Just what do you want?"

"A little adventure. Some fun and romance maybe." Her face turned sour. "Oh, not with you, for God's sake."

Manny looked past her and saw Christine watching. With

his foot on the same step as his ex, he made a sideways push past Donna that put him on the next level of the stairs. With a few quick leaps he was able to catch up to Christine.

"Nice move," said Donna. "Very agile. Have you been secretly watching my videos?"

Christine looked at him as if expecting an answer. He smiled and moved on.

With her feet straddling two different steps, Donna struck her final model pose before continuing.

Fans were going wild, messaging friends and telling them to tune in to the best soap opera they had seen in ages.

"My marriage had become as lifeless as the stone I'm walking on. A little bell went off inside me telling me to get out of the house and live again. But what to do? Well, as I was saying, Paris was a short train ride away. At first I just wanted to check out the city, but as fate would have it, it was there I met my second husband."

"And the count is on," muttered Manny.

"What was that, dear?" asked Donna.

A drone hovered beside her projecting an image of Manny as he said, "and the count is on." The artificial intelligence did what it was programmed to do. It modified his facial features slightly and the inflection of his voice to make it sound bitter and spiteful. Donna smiled at the result.

"No truer words were spoken," she said. "Yes, I finally managed to divorce my drippy husband and exchange him for a real Count. For a short time in my life I was known as the Contessa Donna Pallatzio DuLac, the beautiful and elegant bride of the Count Jaques DuLac of Maison, France. I have since dropped that title. I think they are so pretentious and egotistical, in conflict with my humble self image." She paused for effect again. "Anyway, we lived in a castle. It was fairy tale cute. We had maids and butlers and gardeners, pool boys, and all the accompanying luxury. I was in love with the Count and he was mad about me. He encouraged me to work on my modeling career." She stopped for a moment. "Funny. He never worked, yet he wanted me to. It all makes sense now. Why we finally divorced."

The artificial intelligence was doing its job, splicing in images of the Count, their dramatic wedding, and the tragic aftermath. "While I was busy with a shoot, he was usually busy with another model. I confronted him and all he could say was he was French, polyamorous, and that his culture had a history of this kind of behavior. I wasn't buying it. He never called it cheating, but that's what it was, plain and simple. So disrespectful! Who wants to be a cuckold? Well, I did what any woman would. I talked with friends, met with some lawyers, and got some good advice. I didn't want his money. I was making enough on my own, but the courts still awarded me a substantial sum of his estate. As with my first husband, I moved on.

"I can't recall how it exactly happened, but I found myself engaged to Richard Sooka, the famous clothes designer. You probably remember that he was a judge on the show *Designer Derby*. You may also remember that he was brutally murdered by one of the disgruntled contestants along with Haille Crumstein, the show's hostess. My good friend Julie Ann Carver wrote a loose story all about it. I told her I didn't want to be in it, but she couldn't stop from mentioning me."

Artificial Intelligence spliced in images of Julie Ann Carver, flashes of her career, her literary achievements, and her work with world leaders. There were pictures with her beside President Carson Whiteweather and another with T. Harmon Rothschild, the richest man in the world. Finally there was a blaze of fire and the cover of the novel Donna was talking about appeared, *Case of the Missing Dick*. Review texts popped on the screen: *Bizarre. A journey through a lunatic's self imposed hell. A critique on reality shows. A veritable scream for help.* The book opened, compelling passages placed before the audience, subtly marketing the book. The AI adjusted the passages to appeal to the profile registered to the account. The fans had been asked plenty of questions when they signed up to gain access to Donna's site. The AI knew them all well. At the speed of electrons it was tailoring passages from the book to appeal to individual tastes.

The commercial was over. Donna finally resumed talking. "After more legal maneuvering, I inherited most of Dick's enterprises including his design house and sweatshops. Naturally I freed his workers from slave wages, introduced my own fashion line, and gradually rose to become the successful woman and role model I am today."

With one graceful lift of her leg she climbed the final step. With the magnificent view behind her, the intricacies of New Maya City of Worlds and her face lit by the morning sun, she struck yet another model pose saying, "And here I am, at the top of my game."

The image projected to millions of viewers, made even more stunning as the Artificial Intelligence directed a battery of other intelligences, computerized artists and writers working hard to enhance the experience.

Donna turned to explore the top of the pyramid, humming softly, the drones circling around her like birds playfully circling a Disney princess.

Barnheart was sitting on a wooden bench, the children beside him. They all had long faces.

"Where is everyone?" she asked.

"Over there," said Barnheart. "Trying to get past another guard. Randall has a writ granting him entrance but they still won't let him in."

"What nonsense," she said. She seemed to notice their faces for the first time. AI loved the image of sad children. "Why so glum?" she asked. Before either of them could answer she looked around, saying, "And where's that soul we came to rescue?"

"Inside the pyramid temple," said Petra.

"They won't let us in," added Yorgi. "And we built this temple!"

"I know, children. I know," said Barnheart.

"We tried moving some stones but they wouldn't respond," said Yorgi.

"The rocks are not happy," said Petra. "There is an uproar in their community and they are frozen in fear. They say the temple could collapse."

Donna smiled politely, not knowing it was all true. The twins were unique, blessed with special talents.

"We may have climbed all this way for nothing," said Barnheart.

"Nonsense," she said.

"Even the children can't help us," said Barnheart. "Kamala Singh has done something to the temple to block their abilities to move the stones."

She chuckled at the thought of mere children trying to push a heavy stone aside to open the temple.

"If we could at least get past the guards, the twins could guide us to the Ascension Chamber," said Barnheart. "Our mission is a failure unless we can do that."

"Well," she huffed. "Thank goodness *I'm* here!" After a brief model pose and a smile for the drones, she politely asked, "Now, tell me a little more about this soul problem. And which way did you say everybody went?"

Chapter 20

The Past Revisited

Barclay McKenner floated motionless in an improvised tank in a hastily modified observation room at the Eighth Day Village of the Sun Peace Station. Monica looked through the glass at him, wondering what he could be thinking. He was locked in some kind of trance, his eyes active but his body still and tense. He had been that way all night.

She paced in front of the window. Rampa had been right. Barclay McKenner somehow had crossed into new territory. He had been a dolphin for a short time in his life, something he would have never thought possible. It was a dream for someone who was into dolphin research the way he was. He had been taken by the Ascension Crystal to the Point of Departure. In his experience there, he became a dolphin. With his new abilities and the help of his dolphin friends, he led the rescue that shattered the fabric of that dimension and freed all who were trapped there.

When he returned to the three dimensional reality, like some of the trapped people, he had been transformed. He considered it a small price, one he was willing, almost happy, to pay. His friends returned him to the ocean where he started a family and began life as a dolphin.

Until his friends once again needed him and sought him out. After another high stakes adventure, somehow the reverse had happened, and Barclay McKenner regained his human form.

Monica tried to imagine what it must be like. As a therapist, she had dealt with people and change, but nothing like this. Yes, transgender therapy might be helpful when it comes to dealing with dramatic change for humans, but she wasn't sure. Chief Wiggins had put her in charge of this case, but what could she do? She could not even talk to her patient, let alone prescribe a treatment.

She could observe and theorize all she wanted, but it was time to go deeper. She opened her mind, activated her psychic gifts and began to meditate on the problem.

In that state of deep thought and quiet mind, she began to see a clear path forward. There was a way she might be able to communicate with Barclay McKenner. *Of course! Why hadn't I thought of it before.*

She emerged from meditation refreshed. She gathered her thoughts before grabbing her hand held communicator, her link to the Think Tank.

"Gerald Stine here," came the voice from the other end.

"Just the person I wanted to talk to," she said. "You're the Officer of the Day I take it."

"Most everyone is gone," he said. "Just me and Ravi here. I got a report from Randall earlier. He's in New Maya saving souls with the Cardinal. Other than that, it's a quiet day in the Village."

"Good. Then you'll have time to help me with a problem." She quickly briefed him before delivering her request. "Is there any way you can arrange for me to talk to Millie?"

Millie?" remarked Stine. "What do you need artificial intelligence for? Aren't the Village computers enough?"

"I'm going to need their help too," she said. "Barclay McKenner has a database of dolphin sounds stored in our system. I need to share those with Millie. Maybe she can process that data and help me communicate with McKenner."

"Sounds like a challenge," said Stine. He smiled, glad to have something to do. "Now, give me your full requirements."

Chapter 21

Open Says Me

Manny sat on a bench with Christine just outside the upper doorway to the temple. They were watching Randall try to reason with two guards. He was getting nowhere. Manny had given it a try, but he couldn't say if Randall was doing any better.

In that vein, his conversation with Christine wasn't doing any better either.

"She's so irritating," said Manny. "You can see why I divorced her."

"I can't figure out why you married her in the first place."

"She was a different woman back then." He looked away from Christine, a smile brightening his sad demeanor. "She was real, not anything like the pretentious woman she is now. She was smart." He turned back towards her. "We were doing post graduate work together."

"So I heard."

"I don't know how everything went off course after we were married."

There was silence for a while except for Randall pleading his case.

After some quiet time Christine gently slid closer to Manny and put her hand on his arm. "Like your bad marriage to her, it's in the past. Can we move forward together? You once told me that you wanted me to be your partner and fellow adventurer exploring the landscape of love. Is that still true?"

His smile widened as he turned toward her, their eyes meeting as they peered into each other's soul. He slipped his arm around her waist, pulling her closer. His hand reached for hers, stroking it gently. There was a passionate kiss, although soft and quick, like adolescents caught in a public display of affection. As he pulled away and opened his eyes, he saw Donna headed their way, Barnheart and the twins close behind. She had that defiant look, dusted with hints of anger and impatience.

Christine turned to see what had broken the spell. "Oh, God. Not again."

Donna walked past them, turning for a moment to flash them an amused glance. The drones caught it all before she moved on. The final member of the soft parade, Peter the pack mule, nodded as he trudged by, still wheezing from the climb with all the equipment.

Donna walked up to the guards, gently pushing Randall aside.

The royal protectorate took in her appearance. In her belly dancing harem costume and her adornments, she looked like a goddess to them. She struck a fierce model pose, confrontational, aggravated, and with a hint of crazy. It was one she practiced often. In an angry, irritated tone she demanded, "Stand aside and let us in. We have business inside with the High Priestess Pamala..,"

Randall pinched her arm whispering, "Kamala."

"Yes!" she said. "I sent my Manservant here," she indicated Randall, "with explicit instructions and a proclamation from the New Maya Elders granting us access. Now stand aside."

The guards looked at each other questioning the decision, trying to balance their duty against the situation. One of them finally turned. "I'll go check with the High Priestess."

He left quickly. Donna was not satisfied. She began to take it out on the remaining guard.

"How dare you defy my authority! You have no idea what you are doing. An immortal soul is at stake. When my sorceress sister finds out what you have done, she will use her powerful magic to turn you into a worm and leave you for the birds to eat."

It want on and on relentlessly.

Christine leaned close and whispered to Manny. "Oh, my. I think he's going to break."

"She was never like this during our marriage," said Manny. "Thank God."

Everyone watched as her browbeating and heckling brought the guard to his knees, literally, as he finally genuflected in front of her accepting her authority. Donna turned to her entourage.

"All right," she said. "The adventure continues. Well! Don't just stand there gawking. We have a soul to save. Or something like that."

Chapter 22

Returning to Forever

The Golden Being that had been the soul of Kamala Singh sat quietly in the peaceful garden. Water trickled into a nearby lotus pond. Lush vegetation burst with leaves that captured the warm rays of the overhead sun.

Like an amputee, it felt the phantom pain of the missing piece. There was nothing else to do but contemplate the results of everyone's thoughts and actions. The soul remains blameless through the act of forgiveness. There is only cause and effect in the realms governed by karma.

Ixpetz and Papitl appeared before the Being.

"Before you speak, I know your concerns," said the Golden Being.

"You are our soul," said Ixpetz. "You know all."

"Perhaps," said the Being. "Can you believe that like you, a soul is still learning and growing?"

"You know what Singh has done?"

"Of course."

"And you just let it happen?" asked Ixpetz.

"You know the rules," said the Being. "Earth is a neutral ground, a free will planet. I can create humans, give them a piece of myself, but it is sometimes hard to control them from afar like this. Also a soul can easily be distracted by other incarnations that we are also trying to manage. I put a lot of effort into Singh, and perhaps that is the problem."

"But what will happen to us now that she has separated herself from us?" asked Papitl. "Are we not also a part of her, even if only a past incarnation?"

"I'm not sure," said the Being. "Even as I am your soul and the source of your life, there are things I do not know."

Papaitl and Ixpetz looked at each other. Ixpetz asked his soul, "Why did you change Cameron Singh? Why did you turn our brother into our sister?"

"Because I had the opportunity. When I found him in the garden with me, somehow crossed through dimensions and trapped in the Point of Departure, I had a thought. I wanted to play. I wondered if I had made a mistake in creating him. A reincarnated Atlantean with full knowledge of his past lives! I even gave him access to all his psychic gifts, including the ability to astral travel. Very dangerous and daring. These things fed his spirit but he also developed a huge ego, so much so that he challenged me. I saw an opportunity to easily correct my mistake. I had hoped that as a woman, Kamala Singh would be less focused on her ego. I made other modifications as well, but these obviously did not take hold. She still challenges me."

Papitl asked again, "All this is good, but what will happen to us now?"

"I can't exactly say," said the Being. "Time is not linear as you perceive it. It is different for a soul. In the stream of time we can see many things. What happens in one lifetime affects another. Improving the state of one incarnation can improve them all. But it is a balanced situation. If I remove a weight from one lifetime it will shift the burden to another. If I focus too hard on one life I may lose the perspective on another. It's quite complicated balancing the energy at my level, the level of the Soul."

The Golden Being looked at his children. Their worry was his worry. The worry was his creation. He had no choice but to embrace it.

The Being opened its arms revealing a heart that glowed with the Light of the Infinite. Papaitl and Ixpetz entered that Light, joining again with their soul. Their consciousness grew until they merged in knowingness, realizing they had been the Golden Being all along as well as each other. Two perspectives of the same thing, now seen as one of many perspectives. A great truth, once hidden from Papaitl and Ixpetz, was now revealed. Free of their limitations, they flowed in spiritual abundance.

Perhaps the eye of the Soul is more like an insect's. It has the ability to see and process many images at once and form them into a cohesive Whole.

Chapter 23

Salvation Awaits All Who Ask For It

Jameson leaned forward over the prone body. He stared into empty eyes. "Singh. If you're in there, hear me! You've been my friend ever since I came to the Eighth Day Village of the Sun. You taught me things I would have never considered. You helped me learn about religion and God and the many ways people of the world think and worship. Do you remember these things? I need you, my friend. Despite all that we shared I still have many questions."

The empty husk of Kamala Singh did not answer him. He looked over at the Ascension Crystal for help but it too did not answer him. "Papaitl! Ixpetz! What do I do now?" he shouted.

The chamber remained quiet. Candlelight flickered against the walls.

"I don't know what to do," he said aloud. He looked up, as if he could see the heavens through the stone ceiling. "This is something new to me."

He got up and walked over to the Crystal. "You did this," he said. "You can un-do it." He hit it with his fist. "You hard, stubborn piece of stone!" He turned away from it in frustration. "If only I knew what to do." He looked down at Singh. "Maybe you know, but how can you tell me?"

He heard the voice of Tlacoocelotl in his head. *I told you! Do what you normally do*, it said. *You have saved souls before, haven't you?*

"Yes, yes," he said, answering out loud. "I know what to do. Quit pestering me." He knelt beside Kamala Singh and laid his head down on her stomach, listening for a heartbeat, listening for the signs of life, listening for anything. He bowed his head, took a deep breath and focused.

His prayers started in the usual format, memorized since childhood and later in seminary school, prayers he'd repeated countless times. Hail Mary's, the Lord's Prayer, Apostle's Creed, The Acts of Contrition, and many others. He said a rosary, a kind of Catholic power prayer. As sincere as his prayers were, Kamala was not reacting. She laid unconscious on the stone floor of the chamber, her body remaining in some kind of stasis.

Jameson was forced to step up his game. He stopped praying, quietly thinking for a moment.

"What can I do?" he asked in frustration. "I'm just a priest. I can't work magic. I follow the path of Christ, but I don't work miracles. I'm just a humble man."

You can ask for help, came the voice in his head. *You've haven't tried that yet.*

"And who is here to help me! I'm all alone," he said. "And now I'm crazy psychic too." He looked down at Singh. "I need you, my friend. This psycho thing is all new to me. I need your ancient Atlantean perspective and your vast library of knowledge. I need your help understanding what I am going through." He bent down beside her, shaking her empty form as if it could suddenly come to life. He felt for a pulse, barely there. There was a breath, quiet and shallow. "What's going on inside of you? If only you could talk."

You are here to save a soul, said the voice in his head. *Get busy!*

"I can't do it alone."

Then ask for help! Must I keep repeating myself?

"Okay, okay. I admit it. I need help." he shouted. "Maybe the invisible angels around me."

Something clicked inside his head. He had believed in angels most of his life, invisible beings that surround and help us. Was it that much of a leap to believe in invisible spirit helpers like Tlacoocelotl? How about ghosts of the past and the unexplainable things that a big Crystal can do? Was he crazy to believe in angels? He closed his eyes trying to get a grip on himself. What he truly believed in was an all powerful God that watched over everything. With a deep breath he whispered, "Yes. Please, God. Please. I need your help."

His pleas for help took on the form of a prayer. It was far from the shallow prayers he had been reciting. This was for a purpose beyond two beings in a stone room. The Crystal, through its power, had elevated the situation to a larger issue, one that shook the foundation of the nearby Universe and everything that rested upon it.

There is a cosmic law. If you ask for help, it arrives. If you believe in it, it happens. If you are humble and sincere, help will arrive.

The room began to fill with White Light, raising the vibration and making it uncomfortable for lower astral entities. Angels began to appear, some guarding the perimeter, others hovering nearby ready to be tasked. All the activity caught the interest of the Ascended Masters who gathered around to observe the happenings.

Jameson took another deep breath. He felt a wave of calm overcome him. He remembered his experience in the Point of Departure. He had met his angels and actually spoken to them. He focused his mind for a moment, feeling their presence and silently talking to them. These were invisible beings he would welcome a conversation with. If there was a reason for his psychic awakening, perhaps this was it. With another deep breath and closed eyes, he focused on what was around him. "You have protected me in the past. Now, my angels, I ask you to protect all of us as we focus on what we must do. I don't know how you can help. I really don't understand what is happening, but I know I need help. Perhaps you know what to do." The angels were happy to oblige, fulfilling the purpose for their existence. They need only be asked.

He started to pray over the torpid body of Kamala Singh as he continued to ask for help. Suddenly he knew exactly what he must do. With each breath he became calmer, focusing as he entered a deep meditative state.

Singh had taught him to be open minded. Visions of past

conversations with the reincarnated Atlantean came to mind. The concepts of past lives, astral travel, higher dimensional beings, even psychic senses were at one time inconceivable to him. Singh had opened his mind and taught him things about religion and spirituality that he would have never thought about. He showed him the various forms of meditation, practicing with him until it became second nature. Meditation had made the priest a powerful man, centered in his purpose and dedicated to his profession.

Then there was his experience in the Point of Departure. Jameson had met his old mentor there. Father Kaupon had died years ago, but somehow he had appeared to teach the Cardinal a technique he called the Violet Flame of St. Germain. Jameson knew of it but had not given it much thought prior to that. On the advice of Father Kaupon, he had incorporated it into his daily meditation. He was not fully conscious of it, but it had a positive effect on his abilities.

"You may have lost your connection with God, but I haven't," he said. "If you can hear me in there, Singh, if there's any fragment of you left, I ask you to pray with me, silently or out loud, however you can. I ask you to pray with me. You can't go on like this. We will go directly to Management with our petition. I will call upon God to help us with this problem. Didn't you know that your connection to God is through your soul? Ah, but you were angry that you had become a woman, a godess of the temple, a fate you did not choose." He let out a sigh. "Anger has a way of hiding things from us, distorting our thinking and clouding our thoughts. I'm sorry, my friend. Perhaps the connection can be re-established from the other side. I will ask God above to reach out to you and help you."

He folded his hands and bowed his head, stopping to say, "Then again, if Randall is correct, and God is within you. I will also pray to that God to bring your spirit back. Perhaps it will reinforce the connection you already have, and maybe remind you of what you have also told me. God is within you, Singh. Do you remember? God is within you. You only need find your way to Him."

Chapter 24

The Rescue Party

"Left here," said Yorgi, leading the team down the dim corridors of the inner temple. They descended narrow stairs, navigating the slim stones carefully. There were restrictions, tight crevices to traverse, and unexpected traps.

Drones continued to circle Donna, recording things but unable to broadcast through the thick walls. Peter noted it on his hand held device but didn't say anything. He stressed over it, knowing he would be blamed for the interruption in service. Artificial Intelligence took advantage of the communication blackout, drawing out the drama by suggesting what might be going on inside the temple. It presented religious and philosophical information about souls, restating the mission Donna was on. There were animations of God, a soul, and a disconnected body. It replayed the footage of her climbing the temple steps and confronting the guards.

Peter was lost in his device when he felt a small hand grip him.

"Don't go that way," said Petra, tugging on his arm. "Come on! You're the last in line, Mr. Coterie. Let's keep up with the others."

Peter looked up from his device. "Huh? What's wrong?" he asked.

"You were about to take a wrong turn and go down those stairs. You should pay attention. They end suddenly and drop into a chute where you get dumped outside the temple."

"How do you know that?" asked Peter.

"We told you. Yorgi and I built this temple. That's why we're here. That's why we are needed to guide you."

His voice shifted to an adult talking to a simple child, the words slow and condescending, filled with disbelief. "Oh, so you and your brother built this?"

"It's not a game"This is a modern copy of the original temple," she said in a serious tone. "It had an inner maze just like this. Like life, it is a puzzle to solve. It takes twists and turns, goes up and down, and has many choices. If you are lucky and find your way to the prize, you arrive at the Ascension Chamber."

"And what happens there?"

"You get to use the Crystal, of course. In times past only one person a year was allowed the chance to solve this puzzle. Seekers would compete in games to see who would get to try. Winners entered at the top where we did. Legend tells us there were some who never found their way to the Chamber of the Ascension Crystal."

"What can the Crystal do?"

"Many things," said Petra. "It took Yorgi and I to another dimension, a place where we learned how to make this temple. Look what it did now. Someone's soul is at stake."

"So I heard," said Peter. "I don't exactly understand. I'm just a glorified baggage carrier."

She gently took his hand and led him through the temple. He could feel the love coming from her, flowing like light from her heart, down her arm and up his sleeve. He put his hand held device away, no longer concerned with his trivial worries. Every now and then he would look down at her and she would smile back. Though he was single and childless, he began to understand the joys that parenthood could bring.

Randall was the first to reach the door of the Ascension Chamber. Guards blocked him. "How did you get in here?" asked Tubork.

Donna gently moved Randall aside and confronted the guard. "Do you not recognize me?" she said, playing her role to the hilt.

Tubork stared into her face. It was the second guard,

Gronk, who nodded and said, "Yes! Donna Pallatzio. Who wouldn't recognize you?"

"Then you know why I'm here."

Tubork looked at her, puzzled and confused. "No, I don't." He turned to Gronk. "Who is this woman?"

She moved in close, an uncomfortable stare as she peered into his eyes. "You are not one of my followers, are you?"

He stared back, his face reflecting his bewildered mind as he strained to answer her. The drones circled them both and his eyes followed them momentarily. He looked again towards his fellow guard and shrugged, seeking an explanation.

"Be careful how you answer," said Gronk. "She can turn the world against you with a single phrase or look."

"Donna who?" he answered.

The drones began to circle Tubork. He didn't know what to think.

Randall moved beside Donna. "I have here a writ allowing us access to the temple. It's signed by Elder Bruce, head of your governing body here. You must give us access." He gave it to Tubork who took it and read it.

Tubork passed it to Gronk who also read it and passed it back to Randall. Donna smiled, baring white teeth that seemed to glow in the relative darkness of the temple. "Well," she said, hands on hips for effect.

"Better do as she says," said Gronk.

"Okay," said Tubork. "You can have access, but you won't be able to get in."

"What do you mean?" asked Donna, her demeanor shifting to anger.

Gronk interrupted, diffusing her emotions. "What he means is the entrance to the Ascension Chamber is blocked from the inside. The Chamber will only open when the High Priestess Kamala Singh wants it to."

Donna turned to Randall. "So, what do we do now, bright boy?"

"There must be another way," said Randall. He looked towards the twins. "What do you say?"

"There may be another way in, but not through this door," said Petra. "We'd have to go back outside the temple and crawl through one of the light ducts."

"What's a light duct?" asked Donna.

"Tunnels that collect light and direct it to the Ascension Chamber," said Yorgi.

"What about you, Peter? You have anything in that stuff you're carrying that could help us get in there?"

Peter shrugged his shoulders.

"What about these flying nuisances?" asked Manny. "Maybe one of them could fly in there and show us what's blocking the door."

"It's not that easy," said Peter. "The drones are tuned to focus on Ms. Pallatzio."

Manny laughed. "Looks like you'll do some crawling, Donna dearest."

"I'll do no such thing," she said. "I'm the Priestess here. If anyone does some crawling it will be you."

Manny let out a snort and turned towards Randall. "Didn't you say Cardinal Jameson was here somewhere?" he asked. "Could he be inside?"

"That's a good question," said Randall.

Chapter 26

The Council Deliberates While the Universe Crumbles

It would be wrong to say that time stopped for the known Universe, for time does not exist for some Beings and places. More properly, it was manipulated to the will of the Council. They had formed out of the Divine Sea of Love and been given full authority, each Being necessary, each representing a different viewpoint. The debate had begun, just as many of the decisions are made at a higher level. Consideration must be given to the structure of the Universe, to the ability of souls to occupy and manipulate it, to the possible outcome of the interaction of matter and energy, the will of the Divine, etcetera, etcetera, etcetera.

At the present, we'll call it a moment (even though we know better). At the present moment the Council of Souls began reviewing evidence to consider, gently deciding how to restore order. In the pocket universe with the rest of time frozen, Cardinal Jameson continued to pray. The Council of Souls simply observed. In a free will universe like the Earth anything is possible.

Viewed from their perspective, the solid Universe and the higher dimensions that rest upon it seem quite different. Imagine a child who sees a rock or a shell at the bottom of a creek. The child reaches down to pick it up through the water. Once she has it in hand, she can study it, pull it closer, even take it with her. Now, imagine that the child is a soul wanting something, an experience in the physical world. The physical universe is the water, a medium quite different from one the child lives in. It distorts her vision. Surface waves refract and reflect Light shifting her point of reference. The shell or object is the experience. After retrieving the experience and shedding the wetness of the water, the soul examines it, learns from it, grows from it.

Of course it is more complicated than that, but simple to

understand from the perspective of the Council of Souls. They received the energy from the pocket universe, observing at once all actions and intents, free of the limitations of time.

Nevertheless, for the beings in the physical world, the story unfolded in a more linear manner.

Kamala Singh was in a deep sleep. Jameson could see her breathing, slow and deliberate, but her form remained lifeless, her body empty of spirit.

He went on with his work, praying. He began to visualize the bright, purple flame in his heart. His own heart had been ignited by the Violet Flame. He now tried to transfer that passion to Kamala Singh. It's high frequency energy burned for all humanity, but he focused it on Singh. "The Violet Flame of St. Germain," he whispered. "A tool for positive energy and change. It is said it can change a person's body, energy level, and bring in divine energy. Use it, Singh. Come back to life. Come back to us."

The Flame burned in the background, surrounding both their bodies and engulfing them in its power, so bright it was beyond violet and almost white.

He began to talk to God, a child humbly asking for help and guidance. "My old friend, Cameron Singh, he never wanted to be this woman. Yes, he had his faults, but who among us is without flaw? By God, if we were all perfect we'd be with You and not in this mad house we live in. And how would You like it if somebody did something like that to You? Huh? Snapped their fingers and you are no longer a kindly old man. Like that, You're now a woman." The Cardinal chuckled, his words triggering a sudden thought. "Maybe you already know about that, eh? Who exactly is Mother Nature? Could she be you in disguise?

"You see, God, that's the kind of question I would ask my friend here. We would talk about it and discuss it. Think about it for a few days. This is how we lowly beings here on Earth try to grasp what you truly are, God." The Cardinal looked down, casting his eyes on Singh. "My own idea of what You are changes. It has come a long way since our early relationship, ever since I became an alter boy. Even now I find that I am still trying to know and understand You, God.

"Anyway, I have prayed to You before like this, a long time ago. I made a bargain and I kept it. Now I ask for another bargain. I ask You to save my friend here. Do what You must to set things right."

He steadied his resolve, a moment of introspection.

"But unlike young Carmine Jameson trapped in a pit, I have nothing to bargain with this time. I am beyond what I know and what I have learned as a priest. I can only throw myself on Your mercy, Your understanding, Your Divine Will. Help my friend. Please God. I'm out of my league. What would it hurt to lend a hand here?"

His passion brought tears to his eyes. The Council, light years beyond emotion, levels above the human experience, entered the heart of the priest. His experience became their experience. For a brief moment they knew what it was like to be Carmine Jameson and above all what it was like to be human.

He continued to pray. "And if it is Your will that my friend remain like this, release her from any suffering. Please. I surrender to Your will. If it be so, take this empty vessel home and rejoin it with her soul there. Either way, I ask you to make the connection between body and soul again. We are nothing without our connection to You. Please."

The devotion of the priest to his friend and to his faith were evident to the Council. In his actions they saw love.

It is said that love is the most powerful force in the universe and that faith can move mountains. In this state, the Cardinal's body began to grow brighter. The Purple Flame in his heart merged with the pure White Light that burned around him. It mixed with holy intent.

"Love, devotion, and surrender," said the Being From The Divine Sea, the mouthpiece of the Council.

They continued to review facts and evidence, their thoughts taking the shape of a courtroom or a community meeting hall.

"Let us consider some other things during this course

correction. The Council will now hear comments from all concerned." They called the Golden Being that was the Soul of Kamala Singh away from resting in the quiet garden. "You created this situation. What do you suggest we do?"

"I have been contemplating that very thought," said the Golden Being. "I have no answer yet. Only possibilities."

In the gallery, the soul of the Ascension Crystal flashed bright rays of colored light capturing everyone's attention. It said, "Order in the Universe can be reestablished by considering and balancing the outcomes. Start by looking at what caused this. I take responsibility for opening the Point of Departure, but it was human action that forced me to do everything that followed. I was simply a tool in a temple. As far as that goes, Kamala Singh only wanted to be free of the will of her soul, not her connection to God. Can we not grant that request and thereby restore order?"

The Golden Being, the Soul of Kamala Singh, bared itself before the Council. All motives and actions were instantly known. "I am willing to birth a new soul fragment. I only wished to correct what I viewed as a mistake."

The Council's reply was swift. "Yes, but it broke the Rule of Continuity. You should have created another incarnation. And what about free will? What you did was dangerous."

"The Crystal created the conditions," said the Soul. "I met with Cameron Singh in the Point of Deaprture, that place between worlds. In this way station I took advantage of the situation. It was a unique opportunity."

The Soul of the Ascension Crystal moved forward adding more comments. "My Earthly form may be a large Crystal, but few there know that I have a consciousness of my own. Long ago I volunteered to bring the divine crystalline energy of my race to Earth where it might improve the human condition and increase the understanding of how energy can be used. Priests of the past knew the danger. In a bi-created, balanced universe, light cannot exist without dark. In such a realm, there are always places of deep shadow and of intense brightness. Energy flows in equilibrium as yin follows yang who follows yin, and so on in the dance of eternal movement. This incident has shown that it is dangerous to introduce my energy to humans. In their current condition they will never master my true purpose. My function in this affair has been served, my mission successful. I only agreed to deliver the energy and the knowledge."

"Yes," said the Council. "And what do you desire?"

"I want to ascend. My mission was successful. Priests of old respected my power, but Kamala Singh did not."

"I only wanted a soul of my own," said Kamala Singh.

The spark of her consciousness had been summoned by the Council for judgment and testimony as well. In the pocket universe, Cardinal Jameson truly prayed over a golem, an empty husk of a life.

Representatives of the Galactics had their say. "We only want the Universe to be be healed and its structure returned to its former health."

Off to one side, a gallery of souls waited for their chance to speak. These were the other entities, residents and former residents of New Maya City of Worlds, affected by the Crystal when it opened the Point of Departure. They had been summoned in their dream states, some aware of what was happening, others experiencing it only in their deep subconscious. The Council focused on them and more testimony emerged, their wills and wishes reflected like sunlight through a diamond.

"I no longer wish to be an animal," said one. "I can appreciate being human and will do a better job of it."

"I thought I wanted to move on," said another. "But there are things that I left undone on Earth. Is there a way I can I return?"

"It was the will of my spouse to become this thing I am now," said yet another soul. "I am not this creature they imagined me to be. Can this be corrected?"

"I no longer want anything to do with Earthly existence. I want to be a spirit guide."

As a changeling at the Point of Departure, even Barclay McKenner was there. "I am neither human, nor animal," he said. "Can you tell me where I fit in?"

The testimony continued until all had their chance to speak.

The voice of the Council answered their pleas. "Any souls who wish to return to Earth may do so. The pull of the higher dimensions is strong. We sense that there are those who are not ready to move on. We will consider all requests for changes from the assembly. Consultations and advice are available for all who seek it."

The soulful wishes were sensed by the Council, absorbed and pondered, balanced with multiple outcomes and possibilities. Many perspectives and time lines were thought out, available for the petitioners to consider and reconsider. Some, seeing new possibilities, opted to continue the status quo. Others simply accepted the advice and the changes that the Council recommended.

And in the pocket universe where the currents of time continued to flow, Cardinal Jameson's words could still be heard.

"Please, God. This man... this person, is a kind soul. Yes, they have an ego and yes they are sometimes obstinate, but these are the imperfections that anchor us in this world. I say these things because Singh, like all of us, is a reflection of the soul. And this is the focus of my prayers. I look at this shell of a being lying lifeless on the floor. You can take her to a hospital but that will not cure this malady. Only God can help her. Please, forgive her, for she knows not what she did. She just wanted to evolve, to become a soul with a destiny of her own. She never meant to lose the connection with God."

There are prayers, sincere and pure, that find their way to the very ear of God. They are wrapped in humility with no thought of self. They hold the magic of which miracles are made.

"The Violet Flame glows within him," said the Council voice. "His request for help is beyond human. It is selfless. We will absorb this evidence as well and then deliberate."

And it was over that quick. There was internal debate at the speed of thought. The Voice of the Council soon announced, "A decision has been reached. The Soul of Cameron Singh will be fragmented and break into two entities. Kamala Singh will achieve autonomy and begin life as a new soul. This is not a promotion, but a granting of divine Grace.

"Most of the requests of those affected by the Point of Departure will be granted, some with modifications. All petitions and wishes have been considered. Let the outcome proceed. Let the energy of time flow freely again. The Council will now adjourn. "

The room, the souls, the Council, and the pocket universe collapsed into a ball of bright light. The light expanded, flowing like water everywhere. The broken crevasses and cracked fissures glowed with understanding and healing. The known universe knit itself back together as bonds of energy, like contracts between light and dark forces, once again resumed their shape, mindful to the will of God and, as God's representatives, the Council.

Time began to flow once more in the lower dimensions. Life returned as the Breath of God again continued its long, slow gentle exhale. To that, one can only add:

Amen.

Chapter 27

Fulfilling Your Porpoise in Life

Millie was the child of Millipede and Badger, two super intelligences that had somehow found each other and produced an offspring. Millie inherited all the capabilities of her parents, including a database of dolphin human language. Monica thought it was more than a longshot, possibly her only way to communicate with Barclay McKenner.

Gerald Stine quickly set up a one way link for them. The Peace Station observation room now had speakers and a giant monitor interface. Stine had managed to do it without using the village computer system. Besides being an independent network, crossing over to other systems was forbidden as a matter of security. Compounded on that was the fact that the core of the village system was based on crystalline technology.

Barclay McKenner became conscious. The madness in his eye was replaced with calm focused intent. His thoughts raced as he tried to perceive what and where he was.

Franklin Van Dorn noticed the subtle change. "Oh good. You're awake. I'll go get Monica."

McKenner heard the voice through the speakers. He searched his memory for recognition feeling like he should know who it was that said that. In the moment between waking and sleeping, his dream became conscious, downloaded like a giant package ready to be opened.

The Council of Souls, he thought. *Was it real?*

The details became clearer as he fell back asleep. He felt reality shift around him. He was in some kind of judge's chamber. The room even had a smell of dust and polish and fine leather. There were bookcases and files all about. A table rested against one wall, filled with briefings, old tomes, and more files.

A kindly Old Soul looked at him from behind a large mahogany desk.

"Have you decided?"

"I'm not sure," said Barclay.

"Now is the time," said the Soul. "If you don't, the Council will decide for you."

"Can I be both?" he asked.

"Perhaps, but then you would be neither,"

"It's a difficult choice."

"We agree," said the Old Soul. He pointed over to a Barrister bookcase filled with knowledge. Barclay stared at it for a moment. There was a row of books behind the glass door that protected them from dust. In a glance he saw them move. An image appeared like a pair of binoculars. In one eyepiece he saw what his life would be like as a human, in the other, a dolphin. The human life appeared to be pretty predictable. He had the status of being a member of the Think Tank. His life plan included travel and a successful marriage. Children would follow, keeping him busy until old age where he eventually slid into feeble mindedness and bodily decay.

As a dolphin he roamed the sea with his dolphin bride Valencia and his child Prospero. More children lie on that path, some with different partners. There would be exploration and growth unlike anything he imagined. That life would follow unpredictable paths beyond his ken.

He weighed the recent experiences he'd had as a dolphin. Meditation and life as an aquatic spiritual teacher was very appealing. Humanity had its appeal as well, a familiar pattern that would also lead to a spiritual awakening should he follow that path. In a moment of indecision he said, "I'm not sure. You're asking a kindergarten child to decide what college he wants to go to. But I have an idea. I would like God to decide for me. If not God then my Soul. From their perspective they can see things that I cannot. They have knowledge and vision that I don't possess. I trust them. I ask them to decide where I might best be useful to all concerned, where I might thrive, serve, and live out my purpose. Where I might fit in."

The Soul smiled. "The wisest decision of all. So be it."

The room dissolved into a million points of light and Barclay found himself back in the Eighth Day Village of the Sun Peace Station.

Monica and Franklin Van Dorn entered the room. Van Dorn dropped his jaw. "He was human when I left. What happened?"

"Whatever happened, we need to get him to water, and quickly," said Monica. "I'll go get help."

She left the observation room and Van Dorn sat alone with his friend. He sighed, then shook his head. "I don't understand it."

Barclay McKenner heard him even though he was still asleep and dreaming. Dolphin are conscious and they dream while resting half of their brain at a time. The other half remains active. It's a process called unihemispheric slow-wave sleep. He found that after all he had been through, he needed the rest, and yet, he was fully conscious and able to understand everything Van Dorn was saying.

In his dream state he learned the truth. He had always been a dolphin. At the level of the soul, his divine self was a dolphin. On Earth he had simply been a dolphin incarnated as a man.

"Are you there, Barclay?" asked Van Dorn. He shook him awake. It interrupted his sleep.

"Humanity is not the only species trying to evolve," he said. The words were picked up by a microphone, translated by Millie and sent to a speaker where Franklin Van Dorn began a strange conversation with his friend.

Help arrived. Barclay McKenner was transferred to a litter and carried to the lagoon where he was immersed in the cool water. He let out a squeal, the water carrying his voice farther than he could ever shout as a human. Soon he heard his call returned as a pod of dolphins appeared. They leaped and

125

jumped and splashed until Barclay McKenner joined them in their playful display. Tourists and Villagers were treated to something unique as camera shutters clicked and video recorders captured the moment.

Franklin Van Dorn watched from the shore as the pod moved farther out to sea. The show was over, and only a few dolphins remained, starting to move towards the distant horizon.

"Goodbye again, old buddy," he said. "Until we meet again."

Chapter 28

Crystal Clear

There was a rumble and the temple shook. Tubork and Gronk panicked. "It's an earthquake," shouted Gronk. "Everyone run."

Randall remained calm. In a disaster, with chaos everywhere, he knew the only safe place to retreat was deep inside himself. Here we are safe from everything.

Manny squeezed Christine's hand. Seeing Randall close his eyes and breathe deeply, he too realized there was nowhere to hide from this. If the temple were collapsing, what could these small humans do against the weight of falling stone?

The small humans did what they could. Yorgi and Petra concentrated their abilities. Using their psychic powers, they were able to extend their consciousness into the rocks. Petra calmed them as she spoke aloud to them. "It's okay," she said to the stones. "Stay together. There is strength in unity."

The rocks heard her plea. It helped that Yorgi used his power to hold them in place. The ceiling above Peter began to buckle but suddenly stopped as the twins focused their minds and used their psychic powers.

The rumble ended quickly. The rock that was the door to the Ascension Chamber suddenly rolled away, giving them access.

Randall, Christine, and Manny were the first to enter. "There!" shouted Randall, looking down at the floor. "It's Cameron Singh."

"And Cardinal Jameson lying beside him." Manny quickly bent down beside the prone forms checking for life signs. Upon gently touching the Cardinal, the priest suddenly became conscious. "I'm okay," said Jameson. "How about Singh?"

"He's okay," said Randall. "He appears to be resting."

"He?" asked the Cardinal, turning to look beside him.

"Yes," said Randall. "Apparently he's a man again."

Manny stood up. He scanned the room, then moved over toward the Ascension Crystal and peeked under the cloth that was draped over it. He went to pull it off.

"Don't do that," said Barnheart, entering the room, the twins close behind him. "Remember what the Crystal did the last time."

"Yes," said the Cardinal. "I covered it with that cloth to keep us safe."

"It's okay," he said. "The Crystal is broken. It's dark and shattered in places."

The Gorgofsky twins stood beside Manny staring at the remains of the Ascension Crystal.

"We could repair it," said Yorgi.

"It doesn't want to be fixed," said Petra. "The Ascension Crystal has ascended."

Manny pulled the cloth away revealing the remains. It was dark and ugly, no longer a bright object filled with light and life. There were long cracks in it, shady spots and shattered pieces of crystal surrounding it. Manny picked one up and slid it into his pocket.

The gesture was not lost on Randall. "What are you doing there?" he asked. "Put that back."

"I want a piece of it for study," said Manny.

"It's dangerous," said Randall.

"Not anymore," said Manny. "By studying what remains of the Crystal, I may be able to determine how it did many of the things it did."

"Are you sure?" asked Christine. "I don't know how I'd feel if

128

you turned into a woman."

"I've studied radiation and particle physics," said Manny. "It can't be that dangerous. I'll take the risk."

"Now that the Crystal is gone, this temple is little more than a tourist attraction," said Barnheart.

For a brief moment Jameson's mind flashed on a thought that surfaced from his subconscious. "It was the will of God and the soul of the Ascension Crystal."

"Huh?" asked Manny.

Cameron Singh moaned, catching their attention. His status as a reincarnated Atlantean with full power was restored. He had heard the whole conversation and as he slowly came to life, he explained it to them. "We all met at the Council of Souls. The Crystal was alive. It had a soul of its own and it was given the option of moving on. It decided that it had caused enough problems and that mankind was not ready to wield its power."

Randall nodded. "A wise Crystal," he said. "And how are you feeling?"

"I'm okay," said Singh. "I feel normal and whole again. The part of me that was Kamala Singh, like the Crystal, has moved on. The Council granted her the right to become her own soul."

"Very strange," said Randall.

"Not really," said Singh. "Soul fragments are created all the time. However, it is a rare event when someone goes from being a live human to an immortal soul in one quick step."

"That's quite a promotion," said Manny.

"Not really," said Singh. "More like a lateral move. Kamala Singh will find that the duty of a soul is just as difficult and challenging as any human incarnation, perhaps moreso. Souls must balance their progress carefully as they learn. I imagine it is like being a spider. They have many legs, all touching something as they work together to balance and move the spider forward. In this case, the legs are incarnations."

"And Earth is the web?" added Randall.

"It would seem so," said Barnheart.

Off to the side, Donna Pallatzio stood quietly, not talking for once, allowing the drones to take in everything she heard.

"You know the drones are merely recording what they see," said Peter. "The walls of the temple are too thick to get a signal out."

"It's okay," she whispered. "We can broadcast it later." She turned toward the wall, speaking as softly as she could. In the background the cameras captured the others going about their business. "It would seem we were successful. As you can see, a soul was saved and our mission is now complete. The temple did not collapse and everyone who helped is safe and sound. Thank you all for following me on this marvelous adventure. If you're new to my channel, please like and subscribe if you want to see more adventures like this."

One of the High Priests of the Temple entered the room, his clothing betraying his rank and membership in the Order. Upon seeing the Crystal, he fell to his knees wailing.

"Don't cry," said Manny. "The Crystal was dangerous. It's a blessing that it is gone."

"It's not that," said the priest. "It's the Goddess Kamala. She is also gone."

Cameron started to say something, but the priest noticed Donna as she finished talking. She turned around to face everybody. Her belly dancing harem outfit caught his attention. "Are you the new goddess of the temple?"

She smiled, taking advantage of his words. "Of course," she said, the drones continuing to record everything. "Can't you tell?" There was that perfect model pose again.

He moved before her, bowing and prostrating. The guards, Gronk and Tubork, joined in.

"Oh my God," said Christine.

"Exactly," said Manny. "Donna Palatzio, Goddess of the Temple of Ascension."

"Don't you think it's dangerous leaving her in charge?" asked Christine.

"I don't think so," said Manny. "The temple has lost its magic. Professor Barnheart is right. It's little more than a tourist attraction now. It's perfect for her."

Guards and priests filed into the room. They saw the high one kneeling before Donna and joined suit. Hands on hips in one of her classic model poses, she reveled in the attention. "Perfect," she said to herself.

"We are so glad you are pleased," said the High Priest.

Christine shook her head. "Can we leave now?" she asked. "I think I'm going to be sick."

"I feel the same way," said Manny. He looked towards Cameron Singh and Cardinal Jameson. Randall, Barnhert and the twins were helping them up off the stone floor. "They seem to be okay and well attended. Let's get out of here." He reached out, joining hands with her as they left the room, a gesture, for once, not recorded by the drones. A guard outside the chamber pointed the quick way to the ground floor exit. As they walked into the sunshine they saw the crystal airship resting on the lawn. Nearby, New Maya City of Worlds invited them to explore what she had to offer.

"What should we do?" asked Manny.

Christine gently squeezed his hand. "Let's pick up where we left off. You know, before we got involved in this crazy adventure."

"Agreed," he said.

In the open air of the midday sunlight, things couldn't have looked brighter for their future.

Chapter 29

A New Maya Lease on Life

There was a flash of Light in the meeting hall of the New Maya Council of Elders. The Phoenix was once again turning to ashes. In a puff of smoke it disappeared, replaced with the form of a beautiful woman. Beside her, Council members appeared again, although not all seats were filled. In the corner, the goat brayed one last time before changing into a human again. Donna Gray, recording clerk, momentarily sat in a pile of straw.

Elder Bruce stood up, no longer a blind old man, now a young virile servant of the public. He watched in awe as things around him continued to change. The beautiful woman picked up a gavel and gently rapped the sounding block. "I call this meeting to order," said Councilwoman Perry. She smiled towards Bruce. "It's good to say that again."

Randall, Barnheart and the twins arrived shortly afterward and delivered their report.

"The Ascension Crystal is broken," said Randall. "It shattered. I doubt it will cause any more problems."

"It no longer speaks to us," said Petra. "The life force has gone away."

"We know," said Martin, another member of the Council. He glanced towards several others in the room. "Some of us have not forgotten, although that moment may soon come. Even now it fades like a dream in daylight, but there was a meeting and a discussion and the Crystal decided, like many of us, to just move on."

"So, what will you do now?" asked Randall.

"First, we'll need a census. We need to assess our human capital. People are a community's most valuable and precious resource."

"I agree," said Randall.

"Is there any way we can help?" asked Barnheart.

"Of course," said Councilwoman Perry. "We'll need scientists, doctors and therapists. I myself could use a few sessions with a good psychologist."

In the corner, Donna Gray started to speak. Instead, a goat like bray came out of her mouth. She covered it like it was a cough, embarrassed and coy.

The room erupted in laughter.

"I mean, I could use a shrink too," she said.

Chapter 30

Loose Ends

The crystal ship stood ready for departure. Manny and Cardinal Jameson helped Peter unload the last of Donna's things from the baggage compartment, transferring them to a convenient aircar.

"At least you won't need to carry these things by hand," said Jameson.

"Thanks," said Peter. "I guess that's it then."

"What about these two big cases left in the compartment?" said Manny. He heard a familiar buzzing sound, suddenly distracted as a small drone circled him. Donna appeared as if materializing out of thin air. It was all a trick of photography and projections. She actually stepped out from behind the crystal ship.

"What do you want now?" asked Manny.

"We have unfinished business," she said. "I told you at the airport."

"I don't care anymore, Donna."

"But aren't you at least curious about it?"

"No!" said Manny. "I have better things to do with my life."

"For God's sake, don't be an ass for once."

Manny was about to retort when Peter said, "Okay, Ms. Palatzio. Everything is unloaded except the two trunks marked for your ex. I'll bring everything else to your new quarters."

"Thank you Peter," she said, condescending as always. "As for you, little man," she said, turning towards Manny. "Our business is simple. I left something for you."

134

"Oh?" said Manny.

"By the surprised look on your face I can see you're intrigued."

The drones and the AI also thought so. They didn't need to edit anything. Pure human drama. And despite Donna's pretense of secrecy about their business, the scene was being broadcast live. The moment was drawn out as millions of fans, like Manny, hinged on her next words.

He stared at her, waiting for her to say something.

Instead she smiled, teeth gleaming as always, nodding gently towards him. He connected for a brief second, seeing the flood of emotions pass over her like a cloud on a sunny day. Though the smile was artificial, he noticed something in her eyes and in the delicate changes of her facial muscles. The smile carried love to begin with, a gentle look that surprised Manny. It reached out to touch his heart.

Her smile faded when he caught on to it, a twitch of pain covering her face as it evaporated as quickly as it had appeared. She finally settled on her staunch and confident image as the model who eternally walks the runway of life. She turned away from him, her head erect, her movements silky smooth and well practiced.

Christine received an enigmatic, trailing smile before Donna nodded toward the pack animal. "Come, Peter. We are off to a new adventure."

There was one last glance as she twirled for the cameras. Two drones followed her while another stayed back, capturing the long shot for the fans as she slowly walked towards the temple. Her artificial intelligence was already hard at work. An advertisement appeared over the broadcast image: *Coming soon! Donna Palatzio, Goddess of the Temple of Ascension. Sign up for exclusive access at the link below. All major forms of payment accepted.*

Professor Barnheart and the Gorgofsky twins showed up.

"You just missed the show," said Christine.

"Perhaps," said Barnheart. He looked towards the open door of the baggage compartment. "She'll be back. She left some of her stuff behind."

"It's Manny's stuff," said Christine. "She left it behind for him. Part of the business Donna had with him."

"Ah," said Barnheart. He waited for more details before he said. "Well, what is it?"

"We don't know," said Christine. "He hasn't opened them yet."

The twins looked on excitedly. Cardinal Jameson just shrugged his shoulders.

"All right," said Manny. He climbed up into the baggage compartment. There were two containers, one tall, like a wardrobe case, the second low and flat like a long coffee table. He turned toward his audience. "I'm not sure about this. It could be poison gas or something."

Christine snickered.

"Okay, which one first?" he asked.

"The tall one," said Christine. She turned towards Barnheart. "It's probably filled with glamorous outfits."

"And what would I do with that?" asked Manny.

"Well, besides wear them, you could auction them off and make a pretty penny."

"I don't need a pretty penny," he said. The wardrobe case appeared to split vertically, opening in two halves. He fumbled with the snaps and buckles, finally pulling it apart.

"What the?" he said, opening it wide for everyone to see. There was a small, lit screen displaying numbers, time passing in micro micro microseconds. Behind it was a collection of wires and circuits, vacuum tubes and lasers, all assembled into a single system.

Barnheart recognized it immediately. "It's an atomic clock," he said. "Battery operated too. I hope it's one of the good strontium ones and not the old fashioned cesium kind."

Manny looked perplexed. "An atomic clock?"

"Look," said Christine. "There's an envelope taped to the inside of the crate."

Manny opened it and read. "Remember what you said to me years ago before we split up: I don't have time for this, Donna. I don't even have a watch. Well, I decided to buy you one, the best I could afford. Make time, Manfred. It's our most precious resource. Be careful how you spend it."

The twins laughed, a contagious chuckle that ignited a forest fire of laughter. Manny carefully buttoned it up. "It will make a nice addition to the quantum physics lab," he said. He opened the second one, this time recognizing the contents. "Lasers," he said. He picked one up. "Oh my God! Is this one of those compact Omega lasers?"

"We could use that to study states of matter," said Barnheart.

Manny put it back. "There are four other lasers in here," he said. "This looks like a CO_2 laser. And this one says it's an alexandrite laser." He looked perplexed.

"Fine if you need hair removal," said Christine. "Look! Another note."

Manny retrieved it and read. "You always made light of me, so here you go. Now that I'm gone, try these for a change of pace. Donna." He looked up from the note. "Well. I don't know what to say."

"Then say thank you," said Petra. "It's what I always say when I get a nice gift."

"Yes" he said. "Thank you, Donna. Thank you very much."

His eye caught something, a tiny drone that had been watching a close distance away. He swatted at it and it turned and ran, flying away and back towards Peter and his pack of baggage.

"I hope that's the last of them," he said. "I'm tired of being on a reality show."

He heard a whirring noise. It was then he noticed the small drone that had been perched on the crystal ship recording it all. Having done its job, it was suddenly speeding towards the pyramid, retreating like a dog caught in the act.

Manny placed the laser back in the trunk and buckled it shut. "Well, are we ready for the trip back?"

"We're staying," said Barnheart. "So is Randall. He's working with the New Maya Council of Elders. They have a plan to turn this city into a kind of opposite of Las Vegas. A physical representation of the sacred city of Shamballa, or something like that."

"A true Holy City," said Manny. "That's pretty ambitious."

"You're going to need my help too, then," said Jameson. He looked towards Manny. "I'm staying behind with them."

Manny looked towards Christine. "It's just us then."

"What's next for you two?" asked Barnheart. "Will you to go back to your vacation or do you want to stay behind with us?"

"Not in your life," said Christine, wrapping Manny in a passionate hug.

"Okay then," said Barnheart. "In that case, Randall said to tell you to take the crystal ship wherever you want to go, for as long as you want. It's checked out in his name. Have a nice vacation."

Manny looked at Christine. "As long as we want, huh? What say we go to town and see if we can pick up a six month supply of food?"

"Six months? With you?" said Christine.

"Okay," said Manny. "I'll settle for two weeks."

The twins laughed. Manny closed the hatch on the crystal ship and they all turned and walked towards town. Despite the changes, despite the inconvenience, despite even Donna

138

Palatzio and all her bravado, all was right with the world.

Chapter 31

Wise Council

Cardinal Jameson awoke, not from sleep but within his dream. The colors were vivid, the texture of the world around him taking on a strange and etheric feeling. He knew he was dreaming.

"What's this now?" he asked.

The ether around him took form. He stood before some kind of gallery of beings, although they were all one. He couldn't explain it. What he was experiencing was more like a feeling than anything he could hold on to. In his mind he thought of his Catholic doctrine and the mystery of One God in three divine persons. He figured it was something like that.

"We have yet to hear from you," said the voice of the Council of Souls. "Your prayers have been answered. Do you have any questions?"

The Cardinal thought for a minute before nodding affirmative, "Yes. I have many questions, but one more than others. Can you tell me? What is God?"

The voice was soothing as it answered. "Many things. I could show you but it would hold no meaning. I could explain it to you but you would not understand. As you have heard, it is easier to look down than up, and so it is looking into the heavenly realms and the higher dimensions."

"I see. So, you won't answer my question?"

"We didn't say that. Let us try it this way. The question would best be answered by humanity; by beings who, like you, struggle with that question."

Thousands of voices began to speak, men, women, and children answering his question.

A child's voice said, "God bless Mommy and Daddy and Uncle Jimmy and Aunt Dot..."

A man shouted as he bowed in prayer. "*Lā ilāha illā Allāh!* There is but one God, Allah, and Mohammad is his prophet."

A gentle woman sighed, "Jesus is the way and the Truth."

He heard part of an old song: "My sweet Lord. I really want to know you."

"God is love."

"Eternity."

"Our Father who art in heaven..."

"The Tao is the mother of all things."

"God is the world's shared energy, something greater than us, a feeling not a person."

He heard the voice of Randall. "I am God." joined by many others in a chorus of that common belief.

"Vaya con Dios. God go with you."

"Braman is the supreme being."

A Rastafarian took a long hit of marijuana and said, "Jah is my life and my salvation."

"God is the Supreme Being, the source of all existence, the Eye of Providence."

"The Great Spirit watches over all of us."

A scientist looked up from his research. "God is the laws of nature, the underlying principles that govern the universe."

"Waheguru, is the one and only God, the creator of the universe and the source of all truth."

He heard Djwal Khul. "God, the Universal Mind, Energy, Force, the Absolute, the Unknown – these terms and many others are forced from the lips of those who, by means of the form side, seek the Dweller within the form."

"God Almighty, Creator of Heaven and Earth."

It continued until he could hold no more. The voices slowly stopped. Father Kaupon appeared before him. "Carmine, I

141

struggled with that question my whole life and came up blank. At one point I decided that it was a question mankind could not answer, and so I just focused on living the best life I could."

"I'm trying to do that already," said Jameson.

"I'll tell you a secret. Something from my perspective. I accept that God is energy. We are all energy. God is everywhere, in every atom, every person, every *thing*. So, no matter what we are, God is both inside us and outside us. In order to connect the dots, you must begin by understanding yourself. As the Greek philosophers said: Know thyself. Knowing yourself, it will be easier to, let's say, let down the barriers between you and God. You become One, because you realize that by thinking of yourself as Carmine Jameson, you created something that was different than God. You come to the conclusion that by the very act of taking on a human identity, you define yourself as not God. At that realization you will begin to understand the sum total we call God, which includes you, me, and everything else you can imagine."

"But..."

"Don't worry about all these hard questions. They will all be answered in time. Believe me. Once you break down the barrier between you and God, everything will be okay. Join the internal God to the external. There are many ways to do that. Some meditate and dissolve the ego. Others focus on mindfulness, becoming aware of their innermost feelings and their reactions to the environment around them. Still others take a quick path, doing drugs, fasting, or even invoking magic. As you say, there are as many ways to God as there are people."

Kaupon put his hand on Jameson's shoulder. The Cardinal could feel the warmth, the love. Then he disappeared and the Council spoke once again. "We will now wipe your memory, as we have with the others."

"Wait! You're going to make me forget? What about answering my question?"

"You have your answer. God is all of that! And this is a dream you're in. Even if you drink from the River of Lethe, the stream of forgetfulness, all that you experienced here would still be in your subconscious."

The Cardinal felt something stirring inside him. He looked down to see a golden cord emerging from his stomach that was tied to his waist. It tugged at him and he was pulled away from the Council and into the world of waking consciousness.

The light from the window blinded him and he squinted. He recognized his room at the rectory in the Eighth Day Village of the Sun. *Was it real?* he thought. He quickly got up, grabbed his dream journal and a pencil from the nightstand. He began to write all that he could remember.

At one point, his thoughts started to drift. The fog of memory set in and he stopped writing. "It's okay," he said out loud. "I won't stop asking the question what is God. I will ask everyone. I will hear all the answers again. For myself! And in person!"

He poured himself some coffee and stared into the darkness of the cup. "Can my vision of God be any less than another person's? I must be extremely tolerant of other people's beliefs. Maybe next time I meet someone with a different view of God, I will ask them to explain it more." He took a sip of coffee. "Then I must ask them, is that something you were taught, or is it something you feel inside? What about the connection? Eh? We all have a relationship to forge with the Divine."

He took a another sip of coffee, got up and looked out the window. "Then again, maybe it's about the journey and the experience, and not so much about finding the answers. But it is one of the eternal questions that propels us forward." His thoughts probed deeper. "Another is, what lies beyond death?"

He chuckled, remembering something from his past. "When my mother was on her deathbed she said to me, I can't wait to meet God. I have many questions."

He laughed again, a smile born of joy. "I understand what you meant, Momma! I finally understand."

THE END

We hope you have enjoyed reading this novel. For other fine books, visit our website at halfabook.com

Nick Delmedico is an award winning new age writer. His work includes *Tales of the Lightworkers*, *The Seven Day Marriage*, *Aliens vs Dinosaurs at the Beginning of Time*, and the Eighth Day Village of the Sun series about a futuristic intentional community (*Free the Giraffes*). You can reach him on LinkedIn and ndelmedico@dplus2.com

Also by Nick Delmedico:

The first book in the Eighth Day Village of the Sun saga. In the future we will have intentional communities, villages and cities based on humanistic ideals. They exist today, places where people choose different values to live by. Eighth Day Village of the Sun is one such community projected into the future. Set beside the sea, the village has embraced spiritual and humanistic values. They are led by Baba Randall, a holy man who hears of the collapse of nations beyond the walls. Civilization is breaking down. Riots, shortages, war, and coups abound. A contingent of leaders is headed his way asking for help. Not all want help, some are ready to steal technology to maintain their control over the world's population. Will spirituality win out over the banal?

The first novel in the Aliens vs. Dinosaurs series. Sixty five million years ago giant beasts fought each other for dominance of the herd. One monarch has a vision of a better world in which dinosaurs cooperate and live in peace. But that peace is shattered when hostile aliens from another planet challenge the dinosaurs for dominion of the Earth. They collect the small ones, the children, taking them away to a distant laboratory where they can experiment on them and find new ways to destroy the dinosaurs once and for all.

King Rex finds his daughter is among the missing. As his world crumbles around him, as his enemies circle around him looking for weakness, he struggles to find a way to harness the power of flying without wings. His goal: to send an envoy of peace to the aliens and negotiate the release of the children. Failing that, to take the children back using an army of dinosaurs that have united behind him with one thought in mind: Rescue the children.

AVAILABLE ON AUDIO

This book was a 2017 Human Relations Indie Book Award Gold Winner. In 2014 Nick's wife was diagnosed with end stage esophageal cancer. He saw her through chemotherapy and radiation treatments, but it was not enough. Three years later when the cancer returned, metastasized in her lower gut, she refused treatment. He and his son left their jobs to take her on a final bucket tour. This is their story, a family driving towards an inevitable destination that cannot be avoided. But if you live bravely, there can be many pleasant stops along the way.

A little angel in heaven asks her father: "Do angels die?" He knows the truth, having survived the great war that separated Heaven from Hell. His brother Lucifer expected him to take sides against their Father, putting him in a moral dilemma. He instead joined the neutral angels, undertaking a mission to carry the Holy Grail out of heaven to a place of sanctuary in a sacred mountain. Thus begins a momentous quest through heaven and hell and all that lies between. He will cross-rugged terrain unknown to man; pits of fire, caves of darkness, and fallen angels out to destroy him and his band at every turn. Throughout this ordeal, one question keeps surfacing, a terrifying thought that he fears to face. "Do angels die?"

AVAILABLE ON AUDIO

AFTERWORD

In the course of my research for this book, I asked many people the question what is your concept of God? The answers are in the book, however some of the interesting ones came from Artificial Intelligence. My peers were curious about my findings. No one was more surprised than I as Ai impartially did its job of finding answers to whatever humans ask.

I must thank the countless humans, computers, and teams that worked on and built these systems. Future generations will take it for granted, but we can only hope that these intelligent computers continue to give us honest, unbiased answers to what puzzles us. Hopefully greed, political correctness, and the commercialization of the internet will not corrupt the truths these machines have to offer us.

So, for your curiosity, here is what Ai had to say. Like all interactions with Ai, at first it created a story. The following is from Google Gemini.

Who is God?

The Ascended Master gazed upon the hero with a serene smile. "God, my child, is not a being but a consciousness, an energy that permeates all things. It is the source of creation, the sustainer of existence, and the ultimate reality beyond all perception."

The hero furrowed his brow, his mind grappling with the concept. "But what does that mean?"

"It means," the Master replied, "that God is within you, and you are within God. You are a spark of the divine, a fragment of the infinite. The universe itself is a manifestation of this divine consciousness, a dream woven from the fabric of the cosmos."

The hero's eyes widened in understanding. "So, God is not something separate from us?"

"No," the Master affirmed. "God is the very essence of being, the ground of all existence. To seek God outside of yourself is to search in the dark. The true path lies within, in the depths of your own soul."

{ I explained to AI that I wanted answers and not a story. Here is what returned. }

Here are some different answers to "Who is God?" based on eight popular world religions:

1. **Christianity:** God is a triune being, consisting of the Father, the Son (Jesus Christ), and the Holy Spirit. God is the creator of the universe, the source of all life, and the ultimate judge.
2. **Islam:** God, known as Allah, is the one and only God, omnipotent, omniscient, and merciful. Allah is the creator of the universe and the source of all good and evil.
3. **Hinduism:** God is a single, supreme being, known as Brahman, who is the ultimate reality and the source of all existence. Brahman is often represented in various forms, such as Vishnu, Shiva, and Shakti.
4. **Buddhism:** Buddhism does not believe in a personal God. Instead, it focuses on the Four Noble Truths and the Eightfold Path, which lead to enlightenment and liberation from suffering.
5. **Judaism:** God, known as Yahweh or HaShem, is the one and only God, the creator of the universe and the source of all moral law. God is a personal God who interacts with humanity.
6. **Sikhism:** God, known as Waheguru, is the one and only God, the creator of the universe and the source of all truth. God is formless and timeless, and can be experienced through meditation and devotion.
7. **Shinto:** Shinto is a polytheistic religion that believes in many gods and spirits, known as kami. Kami are present in all things, from nature to ancestors.
8. **Zoroastrianism:** Zoroastrianism believes in a single, supreme God, known as Ahura Mazda, who is the creator of the universe and the source of all good. Ahura Mazda is opposed by Angra Mainyu, the spirit of evil.

These are just a few examples of the many different ways that God is understood and interpreted across the world. It is important to remember that these are just beliefs, and there is no one right answer to the question of "Who is God?"

{at this point I asked for 20 more}

Here are 20 more religions and their concepts of God:

1. **Druze:** God is one and unknowable, but is manifested through prophets, including Moses, Jesus, and Muhammad, and most importantly, al-Hakim bi-Amr Allah.
2. **Baha'i Faith:** God is one, all-knowing, all-powerful, and the creator of all things. God is beyond human comprehension, but can be known through divine revelation.
3. **Rastafarianism:** God is Jah, the supreme being, and is often identified with Haile Selassie I, the former Emperor of Ethiopia.
4. **Wicca:** Wiccans believe in a Goddess and a God, often referred to as the Divine Feminine and Divine Masculine. They are seen as interconnected forces of nature.
5. **Cao Dai:** God is the Supreme Being, the source of all existence, and is often depicted as the Eye of Providence.
6. **Tenrikyo:** God is Tenri-O-no-Mikoto, the parent of all humanity, who created the world and all beings.
7. **Shinto:** Shinto is a polytheistic religion with numerous kami, or spirits, associated with natural phenomena, ancestors, and other entities.
8. **Jainism:** Jainism does not believe in a personal God. Instead, it focuses on the concept of the Supreme Being, which is infinite and eternal.
9. **African Traditional Religions:** These religions vary widely, but often involve a supreme being, often referred to as the High God, and numerous lesser deities and spirits.
10. **Indigenous American Religions:** These religions also vary widely, but often involve a creator deity, spirits associated with nature, and ancestral spirits.
11. **Manichaeism:** Manichaeism is a dualistic religion that believes in two opposing forces, the God of Light and the God of Darkness.
12. **Gnosticism:** Gnostic religions vary widely, but often involve a supreme, unknowable God and a lesser deity or demiurge who created the material world.
13. **Taoism:** Taoism does not believe in a personal God. Instead, it focuses on the Tao, the ultimate principle of the

149

universe.

14. **Confucianism:** Confucianism is not a religion in the traditional sense, but it does involve a concept of Heaven, which is often seen as a moral force.

15. **Unitarian Universalism:** Unitarian Universalism is a liberal religion that does not require belief in a specific God or deity.

16. **Eckankar:** Eckankar believes in the Supreme Spirit, the source of all life and consciousness.

17. **Theosophy:** Theosophy posits a hierarchical universe with a Supreme Being at the top, and various lesser deities and spirits.

18. **Spiritualism:** Spiritualists believe in the existence of spirits and the afterlife, and often communicate with spirits through mediums.

19. **New Age:** New Age beliefs vary widely, but often involve a belief in a universal consciousness or energy, and a focus on personal spiritual development.

20. **Agnosticism:** Agnostics do not claim to know whether God exists or not.

{ Last question: what do you think God is? }

As an AI language model, I cannot provide a definitive answer to the question of what God is. This is a deeply personal and philosophical question that has been pondered by humans for millennia.

However, I can offer a perspective that draws on the diverse range of human beliefs and experiences. Many people view God as a supreme being, a creator, a source of love, and a guiding force in their lives. Others view God as a universal consciousness, an energy that permeates all things. Still others may not believe in a personal God but find meaning and purpose in the interconnectedness of all beings and the beauty of the natural world.

Ultimately, the question of what God is may be beyond human comprehension. It may be a mystery that each individual must explore for themselves.

Chat GBT Answers:

I am trying to answer the question "What is God?" for a story I am writing. Can you give me an answer?

ChatGPT said:

Certainly! The question "What is God?" can be approached from many angles depending on the themes, worldview, and context of your story. Here are a few possible answers, each reflecting different perspectives:

1. Philosophical/Abstract Answer:

God is the fundamental source of existence, the eternal cause behind everything that is. God is beyond time, space, and comprehension, and yet, in every moment, God is present in all things. God represents the unity of the universe, the driving force that connects all life, matter, and consciousness. God is the essence of truth, love, and justice that humans strive to understand and embody.

2. Religious Answer:

In many religious traditions, God is the supreme being, the Creator of the universe, and the ultimate ruler of all things. God is all-powerful, all-knowing, and ever-present. God is both transcendent (existing beyond the physical world) and immanent (present within the world). God is often seen as a loving and compassionate figure, who guides, protects, and offers salvation or enlightenment to humanity. The exact nature of God differs between religions, but God is often depicted as both a personal being with whom one can have a relationship and as a force that governs the laws of nature and existence.

3. Theological Answer:

God is a being of pure essence, existing in perfect harmony with all of creation. In the Christian tradition, God is often understood as a Trinity—Father, Son, and Holy Spirit—united in one divine essence. In other monotheistic religions, God is seen as one indivisible entity who is separate from the created world yet interacts with it. God's nature is both loving and just, offering grace to believers and holding all accountable to moral laws.

4. Existential Answer:

God is an idea, a symbol, a concept created by human beings to grapple with the mysteries of existence. In this view, God may not be an external being but a reflection of humanity's deepest desires for meaning, order, and purpose. For some, God represents the ideals of justice, beauty, and love; for others, God is an expression of the fear and awe we feel in the face of life's vastness. In this framework, God can be both a comforting presence and a source of existential questioning.

5. Mythical/Fantastical Answer (for Fictional Settings):

God could be a powerful, ancient being who transcends the limits of mortal understanding, perhaps an ancient entity who once ruled the universe and has since retreated into an unknown realm. This God could be a symbol of immense power, or perhaps a being that communicates with certain mortals through visions, dreams, or signs. Depending on your story's universe, God might have a specific role, purpose, or set of powers that define their interaction with the world. Alternatively, God could be a group of beings, an ancient race, or a force of nature.

6. Mystical Answer:

God is everything and nothing, the infinite emptiness that encompasses all existence. God is the silence between thoughts, the stillness in the heart of every human being. To know God is to experience unity with the cosmos, where there is no separation between the self and the divine. In mystical traditions, God is often described not as an external being but as a state of ultimate consciousness, love, and interconnectedness, found in moments of deep meditation or spiritual ecstasy.

7. Scientific/Metaphysical Answer:

God is the laws of nature, the underlying principles that govern the universe. In this view, God might not be a personal being but a representation of the fundamental forces of reality—like gravity, electromagnetism, or quantum fields. Some may see God as a metaphor for the unknown mysteries of the universe, a placeholder for what we do not yet fully understand about the origins of existence, consciousness, and the cosmos.

Each of these answers can fit a different narrative tone and approach to the divine, depending on the role that God plays in your story. You can mix and match elements, or even create a completely new and unique conception of God that fits within the themes and world you've built.

4o mini

www.ingramcontent.com/pod-product-compliance
Lightning Source LLC
Chambersburg PA
CBHW060748180626
46818CB00002B/507